MURDER IN DUPLICATE

By

Fran Orenstein

World Castle Publishing

Fran Orenstein

This is a work of fiction. Names, characters, places, and incidents are products of the author's imagination or are used fictitiously and are not to be construed as real. Any resemblance to actual events, locations, organizations, or person, living or dead, is entirely coincidental.

WCP
World Castle Publishing
Pensacola, Florida

Copyright © Fran Orenstein 2013
ISBN: 9781939865465
First Edition World Castle Publishing June 15, 2013
http://www.worldcastlepublishing.com

Licensing Notes
All rights reserved. No part of this book may be used or reproduced in any manner whatsoever without written permission, except in the case of brief quotations embodied in articles and reviews.

Cover: Karen Fuller
Editor: Maxine Bringenberg

Fran Orenstein

Murder in Duplicate
The Beginning

Darkness draped the night like a gossamer curtain as out of the shadows, a thin, shivering girl, carrying a large cardboard box, emerged into the diffused yellow beam of a street light. At two in the morning, doors remained tightly locked and barred against the robbers of the night, and cold, gray clouds obscured the moon and stars, the first indication of the coming winter. She stopped every twenty feet or so to lean against the storefronts and catch her breath. Wraithlike, she crept past the gated doors, her eyes on a red blinking sign in the distance. A fiery ache shot through her belly, and she nearly dropped the box. Dark liquid stained the front of her skirt, like coffee spilled from shaking hands. She knew that if she sank down she would never rise, so she had to keep going, moving toward the beacon. "Give me the strength, God, please," she whispered to the shadows of the night.

Fran Orenstein

Clasping the box tightly, she lurched across the grassy lawn, her thin legs straining to walk those final steps. She knelt down and placed the box gently on the steps below the glass doors. At the sound of thin mewling, like kittens seeking their mother's warmth, tears flowed down her cheeks. She parted the flaps on the box and looked down at the bundles of newspapers. The girl pulled out the labeled pictures she had stolen weeks ago from a gardening book in the library and placed them on top of the newspaper. "I'm sorry…I'm so sorry. Forgive me."

Groaning, the girl pulled herself up, and with great effort rang the bell by the door. As footsteps approached, the girl disappeared around the corner, into the night.

Months later, when the winter snow thawed, a trucker found her. She had bled out in a ditch beside the road. They identified her from the school ID card in her jacket.

***

The local police came to the rusted trailer where she had lived with her mother and the woman's latest druggie boyfriend.

When the door opened, one of the police officers showed her his badge. "I'm Officer Riley and this is Officer Jacobs." He indicated his female partner, then held up the school ID card. "Ma'am, do you know this girl?" Riley backed away from the bourbon fumes and body odor.

The woman rubbed her eyes and peered at the picture. "Yeah, it's my daughter, but I ain't seen her since before Christmas." She was so far gone, she didn't even ask why they had the school ID card.

"That's nearly four months. Do you know where she might be?"

The woman shrugged again. "Figured she run away like she done in the past."

"And you haven't heard from her in all this time?"

The woman shook her head. "Figured she'd come back like she always did."

"How many times has she run away?"

The woman shrugged and grabbed the door to hold herself up.

"Didn't you try to find her?"

"I ain't got no money for gas. I can't go traipsing all over the place looking for the kid."

Bet you have enough for liquor, though, he thought. Riley swallowed the retort and said, "Are there any other relatives...her father maybe?"

"She got a grandmother, if she's still alive."

Riley looked at his partner as if to say, "Your turn, before I strangle her."

Jacobs asked, "Has she gone to her grandmother's house before?"

"I don't know."

"Where does her grandmother live?"

"The old bitch—excuse me, witch—lives up north past Salem, so I guess Rosie took the bus, or maybe hitched a ride. Wouldn't be no trouble for her, she's a pretty little thing. Stupid name though...her father's idea. He said she looked like a pink rose."

"Where is her father, ma'am?"

"Hell if I know, or care. Probably dead over in Iraq…the first war, you know. He had to go and fight. The stupid SOB, leaving us with his mother-the-bitch. I took Rosie and left soon as he shipped out. Couldn't stand the woman."

"Is this his last name?" Riley pointed at the name on the school ID card.

She nodded. "But I don't want them knowin' where I live. They ain't been in our lives for thirteen years, and they ain't startin' now."

"We won't tell anyone. What's her father's first name?"

The woman stared daggers at Riley, but he didn't flinch. "Billy…uh, William."

The officers looked at each other and then at this excuse for motherhood. Riley didn't know how to tell her, but figured it might not matter. "Thank you. Ma'am, you might want to sit down."

"Just get on with it. I ain't lettin' you in my house."

Jacobs said, "Ma'am, we believe your daughter is dead."

Shock crossed her face, but only for a moment. "I ain't got no money for a burial." She slammed the door in their faces.

Jacobs shook her head. "We'd better get something for a DNA match." She knocked on the door.

It swung open. "What?" the woman shouted.

"Ma'am, we need to confirm the girl's identity. We need a sample of your DNA to make sure this is your daughter."

The woman sighed, her breath pushing Jacobs back a step. They thought she might slam the door in their faces again, but she stepped outside and opened her mouth.

They stared at her. "What, I watch CSI. Just do what you gotta do and get out of here."

Jacobs quickly opened the kit, pulled on protective gloves, and took a swab from inside of the woman's cheek. The door slammed before Jacobs could close the box. "Let's get out of here."

***

The medical examiner made the identification through the DNA and fingerprints, and determined that her death was from natural causes. She had bled out from childbirth and frozen to death where she fell, along the side of the road. The military confirmed that Rose's father had died in Iraq. The police upstate verified that the grandmother had passed away a few years back. Notification to the mother went unanswered, so the county buried her remains in a potter's grave; nobody came to the burial but the cops, just in case.

Just ten miles away, in a different county, no one linked the contents of the cardboard box left outside a storefront clinic to a young girl lying alone in an unmarked grave.

Fran Orenstein

Chapter 1
The Present Day

As winter segued into spring, Lily Aaron's personal Armageddon proceeded as ordained, while the gods looked down and laughed. Looking back on that fateful day, if the four horsemen of the apocalypse had galloped down Broadway, screaming and swinging swords, Lily might have blinked and continued on the path to destruction.

The last vestiges of dirty snow edging the streets of the city had finally disappeared with the rising temperature, and buds graced the naked brown trees with tiny curls of green. The sun heralded a day meant for burgeoning growth and the beginning of new life.

Down the road, with eyes no longer clouded by emotion, Lily would wonder how an inane choice between a cafe latte at the Java Cafe and coffee ice cream down the street could change her life forever. It was a simple choice people made on a regular basis.

Although Lily couldn't see it then through her smudged sunglasses, hindsight always had perfect vision.

Lily saw him for the first time in the crowded coffee shop, sitting at a small table in the back corner, sucking an obscenely decadent and frothy concoction while his fingers pecked at the keyboard of a mini laptop. While she crawled forward in line at a snail's pace, he was perfectly placed in her line of vision, eye candy that wouldn't add the pounds. Even hunched over the table, she figured he had to be tall...although, with her five foot four inch body, every man was tall. She usually judged height by where her eyes rested when they stood face to face. Too tall and it might be embarrassing. Lily smiled, dimples etching grooves in her cheeks.

In a manner she hoped was unobtrusive, Lily scanned what she could see of his body. Thick, curly black hair framed a perfectly shaped head, cut longer so it curled around his ears and neck. His dark gray suit jacket hung over the back of the chair, and his muscles bulged under the long sleeves of his button-down white shirt as he lifted the cup to his lips.

Lily sighed. If she had to wait in this interminable line, at least she had something good to look at besides the dandruff on the shoulders of the balding guy in front of her. She wondered if the poor guy even knew he had a developing monk's tonsure on the top of his head. Probably not, or he would have done the inevitable comb-over. She stopped speculating about him and directed her eyes toward the side table without swiveling her head.

Mr. Gorgeous must have sensed a watcher, because he glanced up, bright green eyes roaming over the barely moving line of customers. He hesitated for a fraction of a second when he reached Lily, but quickly moved on because she had averted her eyes as soon as she saw him look up.

There were two Lily Aarons. One worked as an acquisitions editor at a large magazine conglomerate around the corner, giving the final nod to stories and articles for their upscale international women's magazine. The alter ego appeared when she locked the door to her condo and stripped off the fashionable work clothes, donning sweat pants and a tee shirt, the costume of the mystery romance novelist. Lily had five novels under a pseudonym and some coveted awards. Her books had made it to the very edge of the New York Times bestseller list, with her agent negotiating foreign rights. Lily felt the tentative tendrils of success within her grasp, but knowing the vagaries of the publishing world, she refused to ease her pace, so every night she did her "Clark Kent in the phone booth" routine and emerged as Lilyann Allon, author, romantic, and crime solver…at least on paper.

To gather material for her books, she used a very personal and secret research methodology; she watched people and made up stories about strangers who were interesting or gorgeous, like this man…especially when she was playing a waiting game like now. She envisioned him as the protagonist in one of her books, the tall, dark, green-eyed man, perhaps a private detective, who rescues the drop-dead gorgeous heroine from self-destruction at the hands of the con-man killer, whom she refuses to acknowledge might be dangerous. Of course, they would have to fall in love in the end, but she could lead up to that in three hundred pages of nail-biting sexual fantasy and thrilling action. This just might have real possibilities as a storyline, and she would have to write it down as soon as she returned to the office.

Back in the real world of slow-moving lines, Lily imagined that since they were only a few blocks from the courthouse, and most of the patrons of the shop were connected with the law, he was probably an attorney getting a jolt of caffeine before appearing in court. He might be married, but she didn't see a wedding band, although that meant nothing in this era of quick and easy hook-ups. Perhaps he had a wife outside the city and he commuted every day, or he owned an apartment somewhere in the city, or both. He seemed prosperous, sure of himself, and indifferent to the chaos around him, able to concentrate despite the distractions.

He took another sip of the drink and Lily stepped closer to the counter. She mentally stripped off his shirt and imagined black chest hair and strong biceps, probably from working out at the gym three or four times a week. Most men didn't know that women undressed them the same way they undressed women, just not as blatantly. Perhaps he was a runner, and she pictured a tight ass in shorts and a tee shirt—

"May I help you?"

Lily gulped, her fantasy disappearing as she faced the young clerk behind the counter. "Um, yes please. I'd like a mocha latte, skim milk, no whipped cream." She glanced in the mirror behind the counter, hoping her hot face wasn't as red as it felt right now. It was flaming like a lit stove. Her downfall was fluid features that instantly revealed her emotions, and the embarrassing tendency to blush at the slightest thing. She mentally shrugged. What difference did it make? Nobody knew what she was thinking. That was the beauty of her fantasies…they were just for her, and her readers should she choose to turn them into a novel.

Lily paid and moved to the end of the counter, into the line for pick-up. Why she did this every day she couldn't fathom. It cost a fortune, if you multiplied the cost of the drinks over a year. She could probably take a cruise for what she spent on fancy coffees, or at least buy part of a new wardrobe. Lily knew precisely why she did it, though. It wasn't just the taste, it was the atmosphere; the young, hip feeling she got when she sat at a table in the midst of the action and savored the drink; it was the stories she developed from people-watching in a place like this. She smiled, picturing her straight-arrow accountant's face when he saw a line item on her business expense— $1200 for exotic coffee—and of course, the IRS wouldn't agree, either. Not going to happen, at least not that way, but it would show up somewhere…perhaps under "dinner-with-agent" or "printer ink and paper."

At last, drink in hand, Lily turned to survey the room. Every seat was taken, even the outside tables, so the patrons stood around sipping and talking. She edged into a corner and leaned against a vacant spot on the wall. Now he was within her range of vision again. He must have seen movement because he glanced up when she lifted her cup to sip. He smiled and shrugged, because the empty chair at his table had been moved to the next table to accommodate a party of three. He turned back to his computer. Lily sighed and stepped outside; another missed opportunity.

The air, which was usually charged with city odors of exhaust fumes, restaurant food, and the sweet and sour scents of humanity, smelled fresh and clean for a change. Perhaps the rains of April did actually wash away winter's grime. Lily dreaded returning to her office in the environmentally secure building that housed the publishing company. She walked slowly, savoring each breath, glancing in the shop windows and thinking about the new hero of her next book.

***

At the edge of his vision, Ken Braun saw the petite woman glancing his way. She wore a fitted navy business suit, and the knee length skirt showed off her lean, muscular legs. He imagined them wrapped around his waist. The white silk blouse lent a feminine touch, but did nothing to hide the enticing roundness of her breasts that peeked out from behind the ruffle flowing down the front. He could almost feel them under his hands. Ken grinned inwardly. Of course she would be watching him; he had that effect on women, and he wasn't shy about exploiting it in the right circumstances. Had there been an available chair at his table, he might have considered inviting her to join him, but that hadn't happened. Probably a good thing, with the thoughts he had been harboring. It might have become difficult to stand up and leave. Instead, he watched as she finished undressing him with her beautiful eyes and left the coffee shop.

If it was destined, they would meet again...if not at the coffee shop, then it would happen somewhere else, and he would take it from there. Ken finished entering the last line of a document, saved it, and closed the laptop. He took a final sip of his drink and vacated the table. The seat remained vacant for thirty seconds before a young woman slid into it, edging out a man who assumed an annoyed expression. *Tough luck, buddy,* Ken thought. *You have to move fast and smart in this world or you lose out.* Ken Braun did not lose, ever.

Fran Orenstein

CHAPTER 2

Lily took one last breath of fresh air and pushed through the heavy glass door into the lobby of the towering building. Gray and white marble floors, like a playing board for giant chess pieces, fanned out in a perfect square. On the right wall a large black directory served as a backdrop for a long, semi-circular reception desk where two gorgeous young women and a handsome young man greeted visitors. They looked like aspiring models or actors, and Lily imagined them rushing from this job to auditions. She waved and one of the young women waved back, then turned her blindingly white smile to the visitor standing before her.

To the left were the public restrooms, discreet silhouette figures decorating doors that blended into the gold-washed walls, rendering them nearly invisible. Straight ahead, two lines of returning employees and visitors waited to pass through the security stations to the bank of elevators beyond. Lily stepped into the end of one of the lines and fished an ID out of her shoulder bag, clipping it onto her jacket. Several people she knew from the company waited in the line, including her friend and fellow editor, Tory Vega.

Tory was one of the few people, besides her secretary and bosses, who knew that Lily was a published mystery author. Lily had to disclose the information when she applied for the job, but it seemed to be in her favor at the interview. The committee liked the idea that she was published, because it meant she was a good writer and would know what they were seeking in articles and stories. The alter ego protected them and kept her identity secret. Lily saw writing as a career, and editing as a job that paid the bills for now.

"Tory," Lily called.

The young woman turned around and, seeing her, slipped out of her line and joined Lily. "Hey, Lily. Did you get your jolt of mocha?"

Lily laughed. "I did, and enjoyed every decadent sip. By the way, you look different today."

They edged forward. Tory Vega was a black-haired, olive-skinned Latina with huge brown eyes and a generous mouth. "Thanks, Lily. It's this night cream that's supposed to take away the lines around my mouth and eyes."

Lily peered at her friend. "What lines? You're too young to have lines. Seriously, what's different?"

Tory smiled and leaned closer, whispering. "I think I'm in love."

"Oh my God," Lily said.

"Shh, don't say anything out loud. It's a secret."

Lily nodded and said, "You'll have to tell me later."

"Three o'clock in the rest room," Tory said.

"You got it."

Lily had finally reached security and deposited her purse on the scanner. The guard made note of her employee pass, even though he had just seen her early that morning when she came to work, and usually saw her at least four times a day. "Good lunch, Ms. Aaron?"

"It was just fine, Jim, thanks. Has your little girl recovered from her virus?" Lily passed through the detector without screaming sirens going off.

"Yes, ma'am, she's back in school. Thanks for asking."

Once Tory had negotiated security, they walked toward the elevators. "Uh, oh, look who's on line for the elevator," Tory whispered.

Ahead, Lily saw the disheveled hair and frayed jacket of Ted Warren, the company's newest slob and resident geek. Ted virtually lived in the technology center ensconced behind a computer, and never spoke to anyone unless directly addressed. Given such a rare occurrence, he answered in monosyllables or grunts. His social skills were nonexistent, and the water cooler gossips said he lived a solitary life, with his fanatically religious sister as his only companion.

When he had first come to work for the company around Thanksgiving, he had actually had the nerve to slink over to her table while she was eating lunch in the building cafeteria, in deference to the freezing, wet weather keeping everyone inside. She and Tory were in the midst of a conversation when she sensed, or rather smelled, something behind her.

Lily turned and stared at a stained, pink-flowered tie. Her eyes immediately moved up to the face above the frayed collar, and she bit her lip to keep from laughing. Ted Warren stood there, his mouth hanging open, unable to form the words he was obviously trying to utter. He never made eye contact, looking everywhere but at her. Finally, three words…well, sounds…escaped. "Um, uh, Laurel?"

Lily looked back at Tory and rolled her eyes. Tory clapped her hand over her mouth to keep from laughing. Lily turned around again. "Sorry, Ted, wrong flower; my name is Lily. I think you have me mixed up with someone else."

Tory's shoulders shook as she controlled the giggle, on the edge of erupting.

"You're not Laurel?" He muttered so low that Lily had to strain to make out the words.

"No, Ted, I'm Lily. I'm one of the editors."

Ted, looking at the ceiling, mumbled something that might have been, "Uh, okay." He moved so fast that Lily immediately lost sight of him in the mass of people. Tory finally let go and doubled over, laughing.

Lily grinned. "What was that all about?"

When she had herself under control, Tory said, "He thought you were someone named Laurel. God, you don't think he actually once had a girlfriend?"

Lily laughed. "Hey, some women will date anyone who has a Y chromosome."

Lily recalled their laughter, but she actually felt a pang of pity for the poor guy. Ted spent his lunch hour crouched over his Bible, either in a corner of the cafeteria or on the park bench across the street, sandwich in hand, always alone. Lily sometimes wondered what he or his sister would think of her books. The sister would probably wash his hands and mouth with lye and make him read the Bible from cover to cover on his knees.

She recalled the severe, black clad, buttoned to the neck woman in the sensible heels who came to the holiday party, probably to chaperone her brother and make sure no woman seduced him. *Really, like that was ever going to happen.*

Another scenario for a book; messy computer nerd meets siren at work who is found murdered in the parking garage late one night. Suspect # 1, the ultra, fanatical, religious sister. Too pat and easy...readers would know the ending by chapter two. Besides, it was so cliché, and would never ring true.

It was a sad way to live, but Lily didn't think about him one way or the other, because Ted was harmless and didn't bother anyone. Besides, she wasn't a crusader who had to make things better for her fellow man, but she would dutifully file Ted Warren's story away for future use as a character in one of her books, under "Geeks and Other Strange People." Two ideas in one lunch hour...not bad. Maybe there was even a storyline in there that would merge the two ideas.

The thoughts flew from her mind when Tory pulled her toward a different elevator. "Come on, we'll take this one."

Allowing herself to be led away, Lily was relieved to be far from Ted Warren, because he usually had fresh food droppings somewhere on his clothes, and depending on the sandwich of the day, might smell of onions, salami, fish, or some unidentifiable odor that she wasn't anxious to experience. Lily promised herself that she would definitely consider him for a character in her next book, maybe a murder victim. She imagined the people in his elevator would relish doing away with him right now. Another stepping stone to Armageddon, had Lily but known the signs.

Lily and Tory parted ways after they exited the elevator. "Three o'clock at the ladies' room," Tory said, waving.

Chapter 3

Alison Pierce looked up at Lily from behind her desk to the left of the door to Lily's office. "Anything interesting at lunch, today?"

"Yum, delicious eye candy...licorice curls with lime green eyes."

Alison let out a long sigh. "Sounds wonderfully exotic; oh, to be young and single again."

"You don't fool me, Ali; you adore your husband, your kids, and those gorgeous grandkids. You wouldn't trade them for anything," Lily said, grinning.

"Well, no, but I'm not dead yet, Lily...I can dream."

Lily laughed. "I bet you can at that."

Ali handed her a fistful of messages. "You have a pile of manuscripts on your desk; have fun."

Lily shook her head. She adored Ali and considered herself very lucky to have such a great secretary and friend. Lily missed her parents, now retired in Florida, and Ali was a stand-in for her mother in many ways. Ali supplied the cookies and holiday meals that Lily no longer had since her parents had moved so far away.

It was only a five-hour drive from New York to Boston when they had still lived in Massachusetts, and she had often driven up for long weekends. Now, it took most of a day to fly to Florida, with the cumbersome airline requirements and security scans. Soon they would all be stripping naked to be paraded through the machines. *Great for nudists or perverts*, she mused. Spending two days traveling just wasn't viable for long weekends anymore, so her visits were confined to major holidays and celebrations. Ali filled the gap, making sure that Lily spent time with her lively family. Lily was careful, though, to keep an outward emotional distance because she was still Ali's boss, although deep inside, Lily loved Ali and her family.

Before doing anything, Lily opened her email and made note of the story characters and possible scenarios she had envisioned at lunch, then sent it to her own email account at home. That done, she sat back and wondered what Mr. Black Hair and Green Eyes would look like in a tight, skimpy Speedo, or just stepping out of a shower, the water glistening on his curly black chest hairs and.... *Stop!* Lily grinned at her flagrant imagination...wrong place, wrong time.

Sighing, she sorted the phone messages and spent the next hour answering the important work-related phone calls. Finally, she stood up, stretched, and looked at her watch. It was almost three, so she opted for the ladies' room and Tory's tale of love. Lily stopped at the break room and retrieved a bottle of water from the refrigerator, guzzling the cold liquid. She wrote her name on the label with the marker hanging from a hook on the wall and replaced the bottle.

Tory sat on the sofa provided in the lounge attached to the bathroom. "There you are! I was afraid you would get involved with work and not come."

"Not on your life, I'm dying to hear all about this new love interest. I might even put it in a book."

Tory's eyes widened. "Don't even think it."

Lily grinned. "Just kidding! So tell me all about it."

Tory's tense shoulders dropped and she glanced around to make sure they were alone. The words rushed out. "He's an actuary. Do you believe it? And his family is from Puerto Rico, like my family. My mother's dream son-in-law—"

"Hold on, it's gotten as far as your parents? How could you keep it a secret from me?"

"No, no, you don't understand...they don't know anything about him yet. It's just that I know my mother, and me having a Puerto Rican boyfriend is like you bringing home a Jewish doctor to your mother. Not that my mother cares about his career...just that he's in the same ethnic group and educated."

Lily laughed until she couldn't breathe. Finally, she got herself under control and gasped, "I get the picture. My mother would probably call a wedding planner the next day and make an appointment at the bridal shop, after she made her plane reservations to come up here."

Tory grinned. "You are not alone, my friend. My mother will start calling salsa bands before anything else, then worry about the wedding. You know, music before food."

The room rang with their laughter.

"So how did you meet him?"

"Don't you dare say a word. I met him on-line."

Lily bit her lip to keep from reacting.

"Well, we're not all gorgeous and petite like you, Lily. Some of us need help in that department; and besides, my cousin met her husband that way, and they're very happy."

"Who am I to say anything? I'm not exactly fending off the men right now. My mother actually said the words 'dating service' the other day. Of course, she heard it from someone in her mahjong gang, whose husband's third cousin's son met his second wife that way. At least, I think that was the six degrees of separation."

Laughter echoed off the tiled walls. Choking back a giggle, Tory said, "I have to get back to work. Let's have lunch one day this week and I'll tell you more."

All that laughter and the half a bottle of water sent Lily to the toilet. Once she washed, she returned to the break room and retrieved the rest of the water from the refrigerator. She looked at it doubtfully, wondering if a strange mouth had touched the rim. Just to be sure, she opened it and washed the rim and cap, then dried it off and returned to her office. Ali was away from her desk, probably on break.

Lily flipped through the manuscripts and set them aside for later. Her email held four new articles from the editorial staff for her approval or rejection, and twelve direct queries to her email account; didn't people ever check the submissions requirements? Those she immediately shunted off to the editorial staff, and filed the others in an email folder marked "Articles for Acceptance/Rejection" for review the next morning. She had a strict routine and tried not to upset the cart by doing things out of order, because then her personal "Mist of the Overwhelming Worksite" would descend and engulf her in stress.

Mornings meant submission reviews from the editorial staff, and afternoons she spent on the phone and email messaging. Today, however, the manuscripts beckoned from the in basket and she glanced at her watch. It had been a slow day, so she picked up the top submission for a short story and began to read.

Fran Orenstein

CHAPTER 4

Two days later, Lily saw him again. As she raced around the corner, running late because she'd missed her regular subway train and the line at the bagel shop was out the door, she saw him entering a building across the street. At least she thought it was him, because all she saw was his back and those beautiful black curls. She made note of the address. From previous exploration with Tory, she knew that two large law firms took up most of the building, along with a big accounting firm and a smattering of smaller businesses.

He could be an accountant, but she hoped not. Her last very short-lived relationship—if you could call five dates a relationship—was an auditor, and as boring as vanilla ice cream when he actually said something. Mostly he just sat and nodded, but he was good-looking. *Shows you can't tell a book by the flashy cover*, so she had shelved him after five pages.

Stop this, Lily Aaron, you've never even talked to the Adonis in black curls...he could be equally boring. It was unfair and politically incorrect of her, because she only knew the one accountant; and besides, who said lawyers were any more exciting than accountants? All through the morning, Mr. Adonis kept drifting in and out of her thoughts, and by eleven o'clock, Lily heard the siren call of a mocha latte.

She dutifully ate a homemade turkey sandwich at her desk, a nod to her bank account and the diminishing returns of mocha lattes five days a week. Besides, it reduced the guilt with every sip of the expensive drink. Then she hooked her purse over her arm, and like a woman on a mission sailed out of the office and joined the lunch crowd exiting the building.

Lily breathed deeply, expecting fresh air, and nearly choked on the exhaust fumes from a double-parked truck making a delivery. It was a New York thing, double-parking, because there were never any open spots on the street, so how was a person supposed to make a delivery if they didn't double park and block traffic? Of course, the vehicles were always left running, as if everyone had one goal in mind…to destroy the ozone layer.

Lily skirted the truck and skipped across the street with a half dozen other people, one eye open for the on-coming traffic. New Yorkers learned to jay walk as soon as they could balance on two legs. Blocks were long and corners were far, so walking all the way down to a corner to wait for the green hand to give you permission to cross took up too much time in the harried, hurried hour called lunch. Besides, there were so many awe-struck tourists waiting at the corners, staring at the skyscrapers, that the light would change twice before everyone could cross.

Safely on the other side, Lily followed the other caffeine-starved people into the store and joined the inevitable line. She looked around, as though studying the décor, but didn't see Adonis. Uttering a silent expletive, she looked up at the mirrored wall, and there he was, standing in line a few people behind her. He met her eyes in the mirror and smiled. *Oh, boy*!

Interminable minutes passed before Lily gave her order and retrieved her drink. Cup in hand, she spotted a woman picking up trash at a table for two and pushed through the crowd like a scythe cutting a swath through a field of tall grass. As the woman rose, Lily slid in and put her purse on the other seat, pulling it around beside her. People glared daggers at her, but Lily put on a blank face and sipped daintily at her drink.

Under her lashes, she spotted Adonis picking up his drink and looking around for a table. She tilted her head and smiled at him. True to form, he approached her table and asked, "Is this seat taken?"

"It is now." Lily removed her bag and pushed the chair out with her foot.

He sat down and held out his hand. "Ken Braun, and thank you."

She placed her hand in his and he squeezed it gently, sending a tingle up her arm. She thought she would drown in his green eyes.

He waited, then said, "And you are…?"

Lily pulled herself back from his eyes. "Oh, I'm sorry. Lily Aaron, and, um, you're welcome."

"I saw you here the other day, but someone had taken the extra chair so I couldn't invite you to join me."

Lily recovered, blushing. "Yes, I seem to recall seeing you here. You were engrossed in your computer." *Avoid looking at his eyes,* Lily told herself. *And whatever you do, stay away from visions of wet guys in speedos.*

Ken smiled, and Lily wondered if he could read minds. Oh God, he was beautiful, and he was speaking. "I take it you work around here, Lily."

Lily nodded. "Across the street, for Brandt Publishing."

"I work around the corner at Hunt, Barclay, Golden and...well, you know there are three more names...at least there were this morning. It's probably four more names by now."

Lily laughed. "A law firm, of course."

"Absolutely! Who else would have so many partners' names in the title? We call it 'The Hunt Posse'."

Now they both laughed. Lily felt comfortable with Ken...he seemed easy to be with. "So, what is your role in the 'Posse'?"

"I'm just a tort attorney. I litigate high-end multi-client lawsuits."

A self-deprecating attorney? Has to be an oxymoron, but a nice touch. "Just a few million here and there, right?"

Ken shrugged. "Maybe a bit more than a few million."

This was getting better by the minute, a sense of humor and smart. Lily liked what she saw, liked what she heard. This one might have potential. She looked at her watch and saw with dismay that the hour had flashed by. She stood up. "I have to go, but maybe we'll see each other here again."

Rising, Ken held out his hand. "I hope so, Lily Aaron. I certainly hope so."

Lily's small hand disappeared into his large one. He held it a moment and let her go, brushing his fingertips along her palm. She shivered. *Whoa, Lily girl, don't lose yourself in this guy, you've only known him for forty minutes.* Before she could stop herself, her mouth opened and the words popped out. "Would you like to get a drink after work?" Well, it was the twenty-first century, and she could ask.

"I can't tonight, I have a brief to work on. But tomorrow night is Friday and the beginning of the weekend, so no work. Can I add dinner to that drink?"

Lily nodded, speechless.

"Good. Trust me and I'll make the reservations. There's a small restaurant down in Little Italy that serves the best northern Italian food you've ever tasted."

***

Lily unconsciously licked her lips, and Ken saw her full mouth glisten, wet and ripe. *What those luscious lips could do to a man.* His hands ached to grasp her curly hair and tilt her head back so he could kiss them, long and hard.

Ken had managed with difficulty not to stare at the full breasts that stretched her blouse every time she leaned back. Lord, how he wanted to reach out and touch them. *Patience, good things come with patience.* He was the supreme seducer.

"Sounds wonderful, Ken." Lily fiddled in her bag and pulled out a business card. She wrote her cell phone number on the back and handed it to him.

Ken gave her his business card. "It already has my cell phone number on it. I'll meet you in your lobby at 5:30 p.m. We can go for drinks and then dinner."

***

Lily walked back to her office in a trance, taking the long way down to the corner and back up again on the other side of the street. The hell with three dates before intimacy, or whatever the current formula was…this was instant heat. She had wanted to pull him down on the floor right there in the coffee shop and feel his hands caressing her breasts and his mouth on hers. And those eyes…she wanted to disappear inside his eyes. If she were a man, she would be in big trouble right now, but women could fantasize all they wanted and not worry about giving anything away. *So dream on, Lily Aaron, until tomorrow night.*

CHAPTER 5

Lily brought a simple but sexy dress to work so she could change before meeting Ken Braun. Ali saw her carrying the extra bag and raised her eyebrows.

"Don't ask," Lily said, clutching the messages Ali handed her and sailing into her office. Ali was right behind her.

"You have a date!" Ali announced.

"I'll take that as a rhetorical question or statement, or whatever," Lily said.

Ali perched on the side of Lily's desk as she lifted the dress out of the garment bag and hung it on the back of the door. "Wow, a sexy little number. So give."

"I met him at Java Cafe around the corner, and he seems nice. We're going to dinner in Little Italy tonight."

"And...."

"His name is Ken Braun, and he's an attorney with one of the law firms in that tower across the street."

"So, what do you know about him, other than his name and profession?"

"Ali, you sound like my mother. How can I know anything until I have time to ask him?"

"Just be careful and don't let him upstairs."

"Yes, Mom. Do you want me to call you when I get in at, um, let's see...what's a good curfew time for a thirty-three year old woman...10 p.m.?"

"Very funny!" Ali looked at her watch. "Oops, you have a staff meeting in ten minutes. We'll talk later."

Lily grimaced. She loved Ali, but sometimes she wished she would retire to Florida, too. Her own mother moved a thousand miles away to retirement heaven or hell, and another took her place. Lily felt pursued by mothers...or was it persecuted? Not much difference, since Ali was there every day to monitor her. Lily wondered if Ali and her mom had a special email drop called Lily@spynet. She grinned, picking up the two manuscripts she was presenting today, and felt the warmth of being loved course through her body, because she knew they both meant well.

The next day passed as Fridays usually did, in a frantic attempt to reduce the chaos to a manageable state so the weekend would be free of stress. It never quite worked out that way. Lily always took home manuscripts to read, so Monday she would not be faced with double the workload. Every day she thanked whatever spiritual guides had led her into magazine publishing and not book editing. She could not imagine plowing through books, although most editors knew within the opening sentence or paragraph if the book had any merit and was worth reading further. It was a strange crossover, being on one side of the desk as a book author and the other side as a magazine editor. She experienced both worlds from different viewpoints, and preferred it that way.

At five o'clock, Lily packed her briefcase and took her dinner clothes into the ladies' room to change. As she was applying her makeup, Tory came up behind her. "Whoa, look at you, fancy lady. Hot date?"

Lily smiled. "Just cocktails and dinner with Ken Braun."

"The coffee shop hottie? So, that's his name. What's his story?"

Lily smiled at Tory's fishing gambit. "He's an attorney across the street."

"And...?"

"And what? That's all I know right now. Hopefully I'll learn more at dinner."

"Hmm...and afterward?"

"Aren't you the nosy one, Victoria Vega."

"Just remember the first date rule, Lily."

"Oh, God, now you sound like Ali. Why does everyone think I need mothering?"

Tory shrugged. "Could it be that you are so sweet and vulnerable that we all want to protect you?"

Lily burst out laughing. "Me? Sweet and vulnerable? I may look that way, but I can beat the best of them, as you well know."

"Oh, yes, so I noticed when you kicked our kickboxing instructor in the balls."

"He should be grateful I pulled back before making full contact."

"He did turn a pretty shade of green."

"No, he wasn't very happy," Lily said. "Did you notice that he always moved out of range of my deadly feet after that?"

Tory looked down at Lily's feet, now daintily ensconced in high-heeled pumps. "Those heels could kill someone."

"Very funny. It's a dinner date, and he's not a serial killer."

"And you know that, how?"

"He's a successful lawyer."

"Uh huh, I rest my case."

"Tory, you are the funniest person I've ever known."

"Thanks, darling. I'll be waiting for your call tomorrow so I can get all the details."

"Just don't call me…I'm going to sleep in."

"Alone?" Tory raised her eyebrows.

"That is none of your business." Lily grinned as she flounced out the door.

"Have a good time," Tory called.

Lily ran the gauntlet of Ali's comments as she passed her desk on the way to her office to pick up her briefcase, now filled with the clothes she had worn all day and the makeup and brush she had just used. Ali was waiting for her, a solemn expression on her face.

"Be happy, Ali. Wish me a good time. See you Monday."

"Call me tomorrow," Ali called after her.

Lily sighed, surprised her mother hadn't called from Florida with her uncanny spidey-senses on full alert. Lily waved without turning around and headed for the elevators.

Fran Orenstein

CHAPTER 6

The evening was a blast. Ken was knowledgeable about many subjects, and managed to push all the right buttons, especially the sex-charged ones. Lily found it amazingly easy to have a conversation with him, while surreptitiously contemplating other possibilities for a happy ending. She had never been so attracted to a man before, and she sensed that he felt the same way. When the espresso arrived, he covered her hand with his and circled her wrist with his thumb. She drowned in his eyes and nearly lost herself until she pulled back.

"You are beautiful, Lily. I'm sure men tell you that all the time."

"Are you fishing for information about my love life, Mr. Braun?"

"I don't even have to ask; I don't think you have any problems in that arena."

Lily kept her mouth shut, trying to recall the last time she had dated anyone long enough to actually consider sleeping with them. Probably that architect Ali had invited to dinner six or seven months ago, the one still getting over his ex-wife. He'd managed to keep her interest for two dates, not counting the dinner at Ali's house. Then they ran out of things to talk about on the second date, and Lily erased him from her mind. Seven months was a long time, as Lily's clock ticked ever onward.

Ken, on the other hand, never seemed to run out of conversation, and he really turned her on. She considered breaking the first rule of dating—never go to bed with someone on the first date, especially in this day and age. What did she really know about him, other than what he told her? Sure he was gorgeous, and sexy, and brilliant, and probably an amazing lover. *Stop! Step back and think about it. You just met the guy yesterday over a latte.*

Ken gazed into her eyes, moving his circling thumb to her palm, his voice husky. "A quarter for your thoughts, pretty lady."

"Is that inflation?" Lily asked laughing, gently pulling her hand back.

Ken sat back, realizing the spell was broken. "Of course; a penny won't buy anything today."

"This has been lovely, Ken. It's been a long day and I'm really tired. Shall we call it a night?"

"No problem." He signaled for the waiter and asked for the check. "I hope I can see you again, and I don't mean over coffee."

"I'd like that."

"Good, I'll call you tomorrow. Meanwhile, I'll think about you tonight."

Lily blushed, her mind on the same subject. *Oh boy, it was going to be an interesting night. Maybe.... No, hold off; get to know him better before you leap into bed.* But what she really wanted was to jump him right there in the restaurant in front of everybody.

Ken took her hand and she stood up, ending the fantasy. They walked to the main thoroughfare and Ken flagged down a taxi. When they reached her building, he walked her to the entrance, then leaned over and gently kissed her. "Good night, Tiger Lily. Sleep tight."

Her lips flamed and she gasped. "Good night, Ken, and thank you for a lovely evening." *Tiger Lily! Hmm*!

The doorman averted his eyes, politely waiting until they were through, and then opened the door to let her in.

***

Lily turned and waved, and Ken returned the gesture before getting back into the cab. He gave his address and settled back in the seat, imagining Lily lying naked and helpless beneath him, and what he would do to her body. By the time they reached his apartment building, Ken was so worked up he was grateful it was dark and no one would notice.

He let himself into the vestibule and walked quickly to the elevator. It was interminably slow, and by the time he inserted the key in the lock and pushed open the door to his apartment, he was even more aroused and intensely frustrated. Soft music and the subtle scent of perfume permeated the air. He exhaled and relaxed, heading for the bedroom, shedding his clothes along the way and dropping them on the floor.

Fran Orenstein

The large platform bed glowed from the soft candles surrounding it, the flickering lights shimmering against the red satin sheets. He sank into the silky softness that caressed his body and sighed. He tensed his legs in anticipation as smooth fingers stroked his chest like feathers, meandering in a maddeningly slow pace downward toward their goal.

CHAPTER 7

Tory called at noon. "Well, did you sleep with him?"

Lily could picture Tory's lips turned up at the corners, but not quite making it to a full smile. "Get real, Tory. Not that I wasn't tempted, but—"

"Come on, girlfriend, out with it."

"I have rules. That's all!"

"Rules? I thought rules were made to be broken. That's what makes life fun, breaking the rules."

Lily sighed. "I was tempted to invite him up. He's very sensual, and he has this way of making me feel special and sexy. I just wasn't ready to go that one step further... at least not on a first date."

"So, when are you seeing him again?"

"He said he would call today, but he hasn't; not yet anyway."

"Then I'd better get off the phone." Tory hung up.

Lily listened to the silence for a moment and then gently placed the phone on its stand. Would he actually call? Half the day had already passed, and she was beginning to regret not inviting him up last night. At least it would have been one hell of a one-night stand...maybe! She really didn't know all that much about him. He'd said his parents died a few years ago and he had no siblings. He'd also claimed that he came from some small town in the Midwest, but had no discernible Midwestern accent. It was more of a slight Southern accent. Who was this mystery man, this gorgeous attorney?

On a whim, Lily booted up the computer and Googled the law firm. She scrolled through the list of attorneys and there he was, listed in the litigation division, Kenneth Braun. He'd graduated from a law school in the south. That accounted for the accent. Some people picked up accents the way dogs picked up fleas. She Googled Kenneth Braun and it brought her back to the law firm and school. He had nothing else connected to his name. Maybe he was exactly what he claimed to be, a lawyer in a New York law firm.

Well, she wasn't going to sit around waiting for the phone to ring. Besides, he had her cell phone number, and that was literally attached to her hip. There was food to buy and a visit to the library to make. Lily hopped off the sofa and took a jacket out of the closet. She transferred her wallet and some other necessary items from her purse into the backpack she used on weekends and headed out the door.

It was four o'clock by the time Lily unlocked the door to her apartment. Ken still hadn't called. Lily wondered if he had blown her off. Well, it was either going to happen or not. If he didn't call, she would find someplace else to have her lunch drink. Another Java Cafe was on the next block, or there was always the ice cream store.

She put away the food and set the new library books down on the table, research material for her next book. Although she wished she had time to read the current popular novels, there really weren't enough hours in the day to do that. Tonight she would go through another submission, and again tomorrow. After all, what else did she have to do with no life beyond work and kickboxing?

"Stop it!" she said aloud, ending the thought before she got maudlin.

After dinner, Lily sat down at her desk with the latest manuscript, but she kept reading the same paragraph repeatedly. She put her head in her hands and groaned. All she could picture were those piercing green eyes and his hands moving over her naked body.

"Stop, stop, stop," she yelled. "He's blown you off." She pushed back the desk chair and marched into the kitchen. The bottle of red peeking out of the wine rack beckoned. Lily took a wine glass from the open shelf and poured half a glass. She recapped the bottle and took the glass of wine back into the den.

She stared at the manuscript. Taking a sip of the wine for strength, Lily willed herself to read the submission. It was pretty good, and might just be suitable for their fashion magazine. She initialed the top of the cover page and placed a purple post-it on it with the name of the appropriate editor.

Fran Orenstein

Feeling better, Lily pulled another manuscript off the pile and took another sip of wine. After reading the first page, she knew the subject wasn't suitable for any of their publications and made a notation on a red sticky for Ali to return it to the author with a stock rejection letter. Then she looked at the manuscript and scribbled some words of encouragement on the cover sheet, along with a suggestion to check out magazines for content before submitting anything else. It wasn't a badly written piece, just inappropriate for their publication. If the author had promise, but was naïve about the world of publishing, she always tried to help. Smart people paid attention, the others just kept repeating the same mistakes.

At six o'clock, Lily set aside the manuscripts and went back to the kitchen. She popped a prepared chicken dish, purchased earlier at the gourmet deli, into the microwave and refilled her wine glass. She set the table for one and suddenly sat down across the table and stared at the lonely place setting. Sadness encased her like a gauzy shroud. Perhaps the wine was making her maudlin, or perhaps it was her solitary life. Tears welled in her eyes and her throat closed. Words from an old song appeared like skywriting out of nowhere. Was this all there was? Where were the clowns?

Her life was work, an occasional friend for dinner or a show, a man she would date long enough for a rare sexual encounter, and more work. Tears dribbled down into the crevasses that had recently made an appearance around her nose. Eventually her clock would run out and motherhood would pass her by. Then the choices would be mama's boy bachelors, misogynist bachelors, divorced men with heavy baggage they carried like albatrosses around their shoulders, or the Ted Warrens of the world. "Oh, God," she moaned.

The microwave bell dinged, pulling her out of the tunnel that threatened to draw her deeper and deeper into depression. Lily shook her head and stood up. The food smelled good, but her appetite had waned. Nevertheless, she brought the dish to the table and sat down. She stared at the plate, and hunger won out. After a fitful start, Lily managed to consume most of the meal and actually enjoy it.

After cleaning up, she brought a bowl of chocolate ice cream to the sofa and curled up to watch a movie. She checked her cell phone; all the bars lined up in a neat row. After a moment's consideration, she put the phone on silent mode and settled in with the ice cream and the movie. He could just leave a message. She wasn't going to let him know she was sitting around on a Saturday night watching television and eating sugar. That was, if he even called.

Fran Orenstein

CHAPTER 8

Ken checked his watch for the tenth time that evening. Timing was everything. He liked to let women stew a while, promising to call and then, just at the point when they thought he'd blown them off, he would phone with some reasonable excuse. They always bought it. Well, except for the blonde last summer. She was a feisty one. Told him to...it wasn't important. There were more lonely women out there than men. The next one would be in the wings waiting for him to come into her life. So why did he feel just a little bit guilty about Lily Aaron?

"You're getting old, Ken," he said to himself. Sprawled on the couch in front of the open window, Ken felt the breeze caress his naked body. He enjoyed nudity and often admired his sleek athletic body in the mirror. Besides, clothes were an impediment to erotic enjoyment like April breezes.

He glanced at his watch for the eleventh time and picked up his cell phone. "So what are you doing tonight, Lily? Do you have another date? Are you out with your girlfriends? Or are you waiting for my call?"

The phone didn't speak to him and the apartment was silent. He flipped it open and entered her number, but it went directly to her voice mail, and he debated quickly. Should he leave it as a missed call and make her wonder, or should he leave a contrite message? "I'll be a nice guy."

At the beep he spoke, his voice smooth and deep. "Hello, Lily. Sorry I didn't call earlier, but I had to finish a legal document for this case I'm working on. It's due Monday, and if I don't finish the judge won't be too happy with me. I'm not exactly looking for a reprimand from the judge or a black mark on my record. It doesn't bode well for future partnership in the firm. Sorry, I'm nervous. I hope you'll forgive me. I've been thinking about you all day…very distracting. I was hoping we could spend tomorrow together. Maybe stroll around the park, have lunch, or go to a museum. Call me back, and please forgive me."

Then he sat back, smiling, and imagined himself undressing her, while a breeze played over his naked body.

***

Lily found the message as she was getting ready for bed. It was one in the morning, and too late to call anybody. She listened to the message twice. His voice oozed sex. Wet black curls flashed across her mind, but she quelled the vision. She turned to the well-loved, stuffed rabbit sitting on the bed. "Let him wait. Maybe I'll call him back in the morning, or maybe not."

Lily awoke to the sun pushing its way around the edges of the window shade. She stretched and looked at the clock on the nightstand...nine o'clock on a beautiful Sunday morning in New York. By ten-thirty she was showered, dressed, and eating breakfast. The cell phone lay on the table next to her plate, set to speaker. She sipped her tea and fingered the phone. Then she opened it and scrolled to his call.

Her finger hovered over the send button and she wondered at the hesitation. She felt caught up in a game of chase. He was the fox and she was the rabbit. She couldn't explain the feeling, but it unnerved her. Lily was used to being in charge...perhaps that was why she was still single. Maybe this was some karmic test. If he didn't answer, she could delete the message and forget about him. Her finger pressed the green button.

"Good morning, Lily. I guess you got my message."

"Good morning, Ken. I just saw it this morning."

"Oh! Well I called last night, hoping you would answer."

The lie came easily to her lips. "I was out until late, and had the phone on silent mode. I must have forgotten to turn the ring back on when I got home." Lily grinned to herself, feeling more in control of the situation.

"Did you have a good time?"

"Just lovely, Ken. And you, did you enjoy your Saturday night?"

"It was interesting, but I would much rather have spent it in your company."

"Flatterer."

"What about today? Are you free?"

Lily considered the question. "I would love to go to the MOMA. There's a new controversial Japanese exhibit, and we could have lunch at the restaurant."

"You like modern art, how wonderful. Something we have in common," Ken said. "I'll come by in a taxi at one o'clock. We can eat first and then see the exhibit."

Ken had managed to take control of the day. Lily grimaced, but her voice belied her thoughts. "Lovely, I'll be waiting downstairs."

***

Ken closed the phone and frowned. He detested art he didn't understand, but to spend the day with Lily, he would pretend. Wait, she'd said Japanese art. He seemed to recall an article about it in the paper…erotica? Was she sending him a message? "No games today, Ken," he said to his image in the mirror. Something was happening here that he couldn't control. Love and commitment weren't his favorite words in the dictionary. He would have to watch his step and reign in his feelings. It wasn't her physical charms, although they were plentiful; she was just so nice. He didn't cross paths with someone like Lily very often, and then he ran like an antelope being chased by a lioness. He was a sprinter, and when the time came, and it would soon, he could outdistance any woman. *Just hang in there, Ken old boy, no need to panic yet.*

Chapter 9

"No! You spent the day with him yesterday?"

"Tory, keep your voice down. The entire building doesn't need to hear about my social life." Lily looked around the lobby while they stood in line waiting to go through security. She wished the Federal agency, whatever its acronym meant, hadn't moved into the building. Then they could go to work like normal people instead of having constant security checks.

Tory sighed and lowered her voice. "Sorry."

Lily told her about lunch and the exhibit at the museum.

Tory tugged at her sleeve as they edged forward. "And...?"

"He was very nice and charming. I had a really good time; better than I expected."

"That's all that happened?"

"Yes, that's all. I didn't invite him up to the apartment, and we didn't have sex."

Lily looked around to see if anyone heard. No heads had turned at the word sex.

"So, are you seeing him again?"

Lily nodded. "Tomorrow night we're going to dinner."

"Uh, oh, third date. You know what that means, don't you?"

Lily laughed. "Is there a rule about third dates?"

"You know what I mean."

"I know, I'm just teasing you. I'm playing it by ear." Lily placed her purse and briefcase on the table and held up her ID. Security checked her bags and waved her through.

At the elevators, she felt eyes boring into her back. She turned and Ted Warren quickly turned his head away. What was with the guy, staring at her like that? It was making her nervous. Suddenly she was his object of interest.

"Did you see that, Tory?"

"See what?"

"Ted Warren was staring at me. He turned away as soon as I caught him."

"He is such a creepy guy."

Lily shuddered. "It's like he's suddenly noticing me after all this time."

"Or maybe he's done it all along and you're just now realizing it."

"Oh, disgusting! Why would he be watching me anyway?"

"Ask him!"

Lily made a face. "I have no intention of striking up a conversation with that loser."

"Then ignore him. He may be a creep, but even creeps have fantasies."

"That's disgusting! I don't want to be Ted Warren's fantasy. That's just...I can't even think of a word to describe it." Lily shuddered.

Tory laughed. "You're giving him too much credit. You probably remind him of some biblical babe, like Delilah."

"Tory! That's blasphemy! I'm shocked!" Lily bit her lip to keep from grinning.

"Get real! Hey, he's still a guy; you know how their minds work."

"I don't even want to think about his fantasies; I just ate. It's like slimy, crawly things creeping around inside my gut."

"Come on, men live on their fantasies."

"If you even consider Ted Warren a man; besides, women don't work any differently."

"You're right, but nobody knows when we have fantasies, do they?"

"I hope not," Lily said, recalling her beet-red face in the mirror at the coffee shop.

They stopped the conversation when the elevator doors opened and everyone pushed inside. Lily turned to see Ted Warren at the front of the elevator staring at her reflection in the shiny door. Lily gritted her teeth and stared straight ahead, not meeting his eyes.

The geek left the elevator first and Lily let out the breath she had been holding. When they reached their floor, Lily and Tory stepped out. Lily grabbed Tory's arm.

"Did you see him staring at my reflection?"

"Relax, Lily. He's harmless. Probably just infatuated with you."

"It's like he's studying me. It's unnerving!"

"Forget him. Think about mocha lattes after lunch."

Lily smiled. "You're right! He's just a sad little man."

Tory nodded. "Absolutely."

They parted company and Lily steeled herself to pass the Alison Pierce gauntlet.

"So tell me!" Alison said, following Lily into her office and shutting the door.

Lily sighed. "Have you been taken over by my mother?"

Alison laughed and parked herself in the chair after removing a pile of file folders. "Mothers are mothers. Besides, I have to make sure you don't do anything you shouldn't do."

"Oh my God! This is like an episode from a soap opera. Are you supposed to call my mother after we talk?"

Alison shook her head. "Now don't get huffy. If you don't want to tell me, then I'll just go back to my desk and slave away for the rest of the day." She stood up and turned toward the door.

Lily sighed. "Come back, here. I know you mean well, it's just that I'm not some teenager."

Alison smiled and sat again. "So…?"

Lily retold the story of Sunday's adventure. "He was a perfect gentleman."

"Well, that's good. I mean, there's no rush." Alison face was as red as a delicious apple. "I'd better get back to work."

Lily watched the door shut and leaned back in her chair, laughing. Poor Alison! Between her mother and her secretary, there was enough pressure for her to find a man and get married that it might just happen. She thought about Ken's prospects as a husband. Wasn't that what women did? Check for a wedding ring—not that an empty ring finger on the left hand meant anything in this day and age. Did he have a good job? And was he genetically up to her standards? It sounded so cold and clinical. The most important part, chemistry...well, that remained to be seen. So far, so good.

Fran Orenstein

CHAPTER 10

Manic Monday, Lily thought, staring at the long list of emails clogging up the inbox. Authors seemed to take great pleasure in sending queries and submissions over the weekend. She sighed and began to plow through them, deleting and forwarding as appropriate. After two hours, she stretched and stood; time for a break and a shot of caffeine, with the other half of this morning's bagel.

The hall was strangely empty; even Alison was missing in action. Where had everyone gone? Lily glanced at her watch; it was nearing the end of the morning break, so they would all be coming back in a few minutes. She was the one who was running late.

Lily approached the door to the break room, when out of the corner of her eye she saw an apparition...Ted Warren slinking around the corner from the stairwell. What was he doing on her floor? The odor of garlic wafted into her nostrils as Ted came closer. She backed away and debated about making a run for her office. Why wasn't anyone coming back from break? *Don't be stupid, Lily, he's harmless. What could he possibly do, except be annoying?* Nevertheless, Lily turned and walked as rapidly as she could in high heels toward her office door.

"Wait, please," Ted called, following her. "I uh, just want to talk to you."

Lily stopped by Alison's desk, her hand on the phone. "What is it Ted? I'm very busy this morning."

"Um, I uh...."

"What, Ted?" Her voice rose.

"Uh...."

Lily took a deep breath. She was scaring him. "Okay, relax Ted. Just tell me what you want."

"I know your name is Laurel. I won't tell anyone."

Lily stared at him. Not only was he weird, he was also crazy. She picked up the phone and put her finger on the "6," the number for security. "My name is Lily, and you'd better go back to your desk before I call security."

"No, don't do that. I won't tell on you, I promise."

"I don't know what you're talking about, but you'd better leave right now."

He grabbed her arm just as the elevator pinged in the distance. Lily heard the sound of shoes tapping on the marble floor. Ted let go of her arm and backed away. Alison rounded the corner and stopped. "What's going on here?"

Lily put down the phone. "Ted seems to have gotten off on the wrong floor. He was just leaving."

Ted turned and practically ran down the hall toward the elevators. Lily's hand shook. Alison put an arm around her. "Are you all right, honey? He didn't hurt you, did he? Sit down. I'll just call security."

"No, it's okay, Ali. He's just strange, and he made me nervous. He seems to think my name is Laurel."

"You mean he just came up here out of the blue and told you that?"

Lily nodded. "I was going to the break room, and he appeared out of the stair well insisting my name was Laurel, and said he wouldn't tell anyone. I was going to call security myself when you came along."

"I still think we should report it. Maybe he has some serious psychological problems."

Lily shivered. "I don't think so, Ali. He has a problem talking to people, that's all. He's been looking at me a lot lately. Maybe he knew somebody named Laurel who looks like me."

"I don't know. This feels wrong."

"I don't want to get him into trouble. It's hard enough finding a job these days, and I don't want him to get fired over some misunderstanding."

"Well, you just be careful, and don't go anywhere alone for a while."

"Yes, Mom."

"Don't get smart with me. Come on, I'll go with you to the break room."

"It's alright, Ali. You can see the door from here. I'll leave it open and you can watch me get my coffee and bagel."

Alison glanced toward the hall to the elevators and then sat down behind her desk, hand on the phone, watching Lily get her snacks.

The elevator pinged again and three people, including Tory, rounded the corner, laughing. She stopped when she saw Alison's face. "Is something wrong? Is Lily alright?"

Alison shook her head. "You're Lily's friend. Is anything weird going on with Ted Warren, that new guy down in tech?"

Tory shrugged. "He's been staring at her a lot."

"That's what she said."

"What happened, Alison?"

"She was here alone, going to the break room, and he suddenly appeared out of nowhere. He insisted her name was Laurel. She was about to call security when I came back from break, and he took off like a frightened rabbit."

"That's what he called her one day in the cafeteria."

"Called who what?" Lily came up behind them with her coffee and bagel.

"Oh, I was just telling Alison that Ted Warren called you Laurel once in the cafeteria. Remember?"

"Yes, I remember. I told you he's been looking at me a lot. I'm really getting creeped out."

Alison picked up the phone. "I still think we need to call security."

Lily placed her hand over Alison's. "Please, he's probably harmless, just confused."

"I still don't like it." Alison replaced the phone. "If it happens again, then you definitely have to tell security. There's a law against stalking."

"He's not a stalker, Ali, but I promise to call security if he shows up again. Now, we had all better get back to work before we start drowning in articles. The deadline for the next issues is fast approaching."

Tory walked Lily to her door. "You have my cell phone number on speed dial. Don't go anywhere without yours, and punch the number if he shows up again. Okay?"

Lily nodded and went into her office, shutting the door behind her. She hadn't let on about her true feelings to the other women, but he had really scared her, suddenly appearing like that, insisting that she was somebody else. Maybe she should tell Ken and he could do a background check on Ted Warren. He was a lawyer...well, not exactly a criminal lawyer, but he had the ability and certainly the means to do it. She would have to think about it. She didn't want to scare him away so soon in their relationship. Lily paused—relationship?

***

They met at Java Cafe for coffee. Lily worried all morning about telling Ken. Would he think she was paranoid, or nuts? After ten minutes of discussion about her childhood in Boston, Lily realized he had never revealed anything about his own background. She still didn't know where he had grown up, or anything about his family. Just as she was about to ask him, she glanced toward the window and there was Ted Warren peering in, staring at her. Ken's back was to the window, so he couldn't see Ted, but he did notice her startled expression. He turned, but Ted had already disappeared.

"Is something wrong? You look like you've seen a ghost."

"Uh, well there's something going on. I wasn't going to say anything, but he's got to be following me."

"Who's following you?"

"It's this geek at work. He was hired around Thanksgiving in the tech department. He seems to think my name is Laurel and—"

Ken sat up straight. "Did you say Laurel? What's this guy's name?"

"Ted Warren. He was just looking in the window at me, so I think he's following me. He tried to talk to me at break a couple of days ago when I was alone, but my secretary scared him off. She wants me to call security, but maybe he just thinks I look like somebody else. I don't want to get him fired." Lily was talking too fast.

"Or he could be a stalker," Ken said. "Do you know anything about him?"

"He's a slob, always has spilled food on his clothes, and smells. He has a sister who's some kind of religious fanatic. Oh, and he reads the Bible all the time. He has no social skills. Doesn't speak to anybody…well, except me, or the woman he thinks I am, this Laurel person."

"Let me do a background check on him, see if I can find out more information. Meanwhile, don't go anywhere alone, okay?"

"Thank you, Ken, for being a friend."

He smiled and enveloped her hands between his. "I'd like to become more than a friend, Lily."

"I know. Let's give it a little more time." Lily looked at her watch and stood. "Oops, lunch hour is over and I have to navigate security. Tomorrow?"

"Same time, same place. Maybe I should carve our names in this table."

Laughing, Lily leaned down and kissed his cheek. He raised his hand and rubbed it where her lips had touched him. "Hmmm! I could get used to that."

"Me, too."

***

Ken stood and followed her to the door, watching her cross the street and walk toward her office building. Then he pulled out his phone and punched in some numbers. When the person on the other end answered, Ken said, "We've got a problem."

Fran Orenstein

Chapter 11

At six o'clock the telephone rang and Lily checked the caller ID. "Hi, Mom." There must have been sunspots or a mahjong game interfering with her mother's spidey-sense...she was thirty-six hours late.

"Hi, sweetie. Anything new?"

Uh-oh. "Not really."

Her mother paused. No doubt she was trying to find a diplomatic way to ask without seeming nosy; an oxymoron if there ever was one. Mothers and diplomacy did not mesh. Judith Aaron tried another approach. "So, what have you been doing lately?"

Give her a break, Lily. "Besides going to work every day, I'm working on another book."

"I mean besides that." Now her mother pushed harder.

"I went to the MOMA last week. There was a new exhibit—"

"Anything special?" Now her mother was taking the indirect approach. Lily guessed the next question would be, "Did you go with a friend?"

"...An exhibit of modern Japanese erotic prints."

Judith cleared her throat. "Oh, that sounds exciting."

Lily covered the speaker, giggling. This was so cruel, but she loved it.

"Um, did you go with a friend?"

Lily bent over laughing. Her mother was so predictable.

"Lily, are you there? What's that noise?"

Lily swallowed. "Sorry, Mom, it's just the T.V. in the background. What did you ask me?"

"Did you go with a friend?"

"As a matter of fact I had a date."

Silence. "So?"

"We met at Java Café, and his name is Ken Braun."

"Jewish?"

"I don't think so, Mom, we didn't talk about religion. He's an attorney."

"Ah. Well, Braun could go either way. So, are you seeing him again?"

"That might just happen. Have you talked to Alison lately?"

"As a matter of fact we did speak on the phone the other day."

"I thought so."

"What does that mean?"

"Nothing, Mom; it's nice that you talk to Alison." Lily changed the subject. "So how is Florida?"

"Warming up, and the humidity is rising."

"Well, it is April. Are you and Dad coming north any time soon?"

"We're thinking of renting a place on Cape Cod in July. Maybe you can take a week off and stay with us."

Lily tried to envision spending a week on Cape Cod with her parents. *I'm thirty-three years old and my mother still thinks I'm a kid.* "We'll see."

"Good, you think about it. I have to run, Dad and I are taking tango classes. I'll tell him you said hello."

"Right, good-by Mom." The silent phone stared up from her hand. Lily shook her head and laughed, picturing her parents doing the tango. *Way to go, Mom and Dad.*

***

Over the next few weeks, Lily met Ken for post-lunch coffee and a few dinners. One night, over dim sum in Chinatown, Ken announced that he still had no information about Ted Warren. "It's not an uncommon name and he doesn't stand out. You, on the other hand, have a secret life, Lilyann Allon."

Lily sensed he was changing the subject too quickly. "I would have told you, eventually."

Ken reached into his jacket pocket and pulled out a paperback copy of Lily's latest book.

"You didn't."

"Of course. I wanted some insight into this gorgeous woman I've been dating. You naughty lady."

Lily's face grew hotter. "It's a mystery." She saw the amused expression on his face. "Well, a romantic mystery."

"A hot romantic mystery. Do you write from experience, Lilyann?"

"That's a very personal question, Mr. Braun. Writers use their imaginations, you know."

"Hmm...and yours is very creative. I especially like the scene in the tiny broom closet. How did they manage that feat?"

Blushing, Lily steered the conversation in another direction. "I'm so glad you enjoyed it, and I know you are enjoying my discomfort. Tell me, how did you link me to the Lilyann pseudonym?"

"My secret."

"I'm very careful about revealing that name."

"Why? Are you ashamed of your own books?"

"Of course not, it's because of my job. It's part of my employment contract."

"It seems to me that they would want everyone to know they have a famous author on their staff."

"It would change the dynamics. Writers would break all the submission requirements just to get me to personally read their work. Other editors would see me in a different light, thinking I'm getting preferential treatment. It just wouldn't be professional."

Ken shrugged. "I guess I understand." He held up the book. "Is that why you're disguised in the photo with a scarf and sunglasses?"

Lily laughed. "My publicist's idea. She said it makes me more mysterious. Goes with the theme, I guess. Besides, no one at work would recognize me from that photo."

"Hmm. So why do you keep working at the magazine?"

"I hope that in a couple of years I'll be earning enough to just live on my income from writing. Right now, this job pays the bills, and everything else goes into savings and investments."

"I knew you were smart."

"I have a goal, and as long as I enjoy what I'm doing, it works."

"So, how did you come up with the name, Lilyann Allon?"

"That was a no-brainer. My mother's maiden name is Allon, and my grandmother was Lillian."

"Got it."

"Okay, enough about me, tell me about you."

Ken dipped a dumpling into the sauce and stuffed it into his mouth. *Nice avoidance tactic*, Lily thought. She didn't give up, though, and sat staring at him while he slowly chewed as though the future of his entire digestive system depended on it. Finally, he swallowed and looked up. Putting down his chopsticks, he sighed. "All right, here's the whole sordid story. I was born in a trailer on a dirt farm in Oklahoma. My father drank his misery away, until he died falling from the hayloft after polishing off a bottle of gin when I was eight. My mother raised five kids by herself, until her heart gave out at forty-five. My older sister took care of us after that. My brother and I worked the farm as best we could, and the three girls sewed and canned fruit. Somehow, we managed to grow up."

Lily immediately regretted asking Ken to talk about his awful childhood. "I'm sorry; it must have been a very hard life."

"Like I said, we survived, and look at me now."

"Yes, look at you now; a successful lawyer living in one of the most expensive cities in the world. You should be very proud."

"That's a story for another day, and the food is getting cold."

Chagrined, Lily ate a dumpling. The conversation stayed on less personal topics after that, like the latest turmoil in the Middle East and the reason bees and frogs were disappearing.

Finally, waiting for the bill, Lily brought the discussion back to the beginning. "Do you have any theories on why Ted Warren is such a mysterious person of interest?"

"It happens. Not everyone makes a mark in the world or in Google."

Lily laughed. "Somehow, I can't see Ted Warren making a mark anywhere."

"See, that's what I mean. Some people are like wallpaper…it's there, but as background for the furniture. They just don't make an imprint in anyone's mind."

"An interesting analogy. I guess you could say Ted fades into the wall. I just don't know why he's haunting me, and I would like to know. He could be a serial killer."

"I very much doubt that, Lily. He probably knew somebody once who looked like you and whose name happened to be Lauren—"
"Laurel."
"Right, Laurel. They say everyone has a double in this world."
"It is possible there's a relative somewhere who looks like me."
Ken looked at her strangely. "Don't you know all your relatives?"
Lily shook her head. "I'm adopted, so I might have biological relatives somewhere I've never met."
"Well then, that's your answer. Maybe he once met a second cousin of yours and he thinks it's you."
"It stretching reality a bit, don't you think? What are the odds that I have a cousin who looks exactly like me and Ted has met her, and that her name is also a flower starting with an L?"
"I wouldn't want to take a bet on that, but it's one explanation. The other is that he's infatuated with your beauty, brains, and charm, and is just trying to hit on you."
"Like some other man I know."
"Exactly, except I have charms he doesn't have."
"True, true. It's those gorgeous green eyes that make me feel like I'm drowning in a tropical lagoon."
"Such imagery."
"Well, I'm a writer."
"I could take you places you've never imagined."
"I bet you could, but I'm not quite ready to go there."

"Perhaps I could seduce you into submission; swimming naked off a tropical island, warm breezes caressing your body, and my fingers circling your—"
"Stop!"
Ken laughed and drew his fingers across his lips.
"Behave, Ken Braun. We have plenty of time," Lily said, although she was ready to haul him up to her apartment and.... She pushed the image out of her head. Then she realized that he still hadn't told her anything significant about Ted Warren. She wondered why, and if Ken was hiding anything. All the more reason to put off the physical side of their relationship. On the other hand, maybe there really wasn't anything more to learn about Ted Warren. Not possible...everyone had a history. She was a researcher; she would do it herself.

CHAPTER 12

The next weekend, Lily begged off seeing Ken, claiming work and a possible cold. Instead she spent Saturday on the computer, first trying free sites and then subscribing to a couple of sites that required payment. It was a futile effort. There was nothing about Ted Warren beyond his address, employment with her company, and mention of a sister. He didn't even have a website or a Facebook page, and who didn't use Facebook?

Then she had an idea. It would require stealth on her part, but she wasn't a mystery writer for nothing. She would have to access the personnel files at her office and hope she wasn't caught. Tomorrow, the office was closed, but the building would be open because the Federal agency that now lurked on the upper three floors had staff working 24/7. If anyone asked, she could claim she needed to get a file in her office that she had forgotten to take home.

Lily awoke to rain spattering her window. Great, April showers, just what she didn't need to contend with. Rainy Sundays she would usually have a leisurely breakfast, read the book review and magazine sections of the New York Times—purchased the night before—, begin the Sunday crossword puzzle—which she might eventually finish by Wednesday—, then do some housework or laundry, read a couple of manuscripts, and maybe Ken.... Lily yawned and stretched, then flung her feet over the side of the bed. That wasn't happening today. She started the coffee machine and quickly showered. She did check the book review section to make sure that her latest novel was still mentioned, and sipped the hot coffee in between bites of a bagel, cream cheese, and lox.

By the time she stepped out of the lobby door of her apartment house, the rain was a fine mist and the sun seemed to push apart the clouds. She chose to take the subway, which would not be crowded, but at this time of the day there would be enough shoppers and entertainment seekers to make it safe. Rattling along through the tunnels, Lily considered the foolishness of what she was doing. Was it really that important to know about Ted Warren? He was probably just a geek with no social skills who had a crush on her. Then she thought about the disenfranchised, angry employees who came to work with guns and mowed down their fellow workers. *Curb your imagination, Lily, this is not one of your mystery novels.*

"...next stop." The disembodied voice made her look up and she rose, heading for the doors.

Lily climbed up the subway steps and paused at street level. Used to the streaming flow of people moving like automatons to and from work, the desolate sidewalk, still shiny from the April rain, appeared otherworldly. Lily headed across the empty street without worrying about oncoming traffic or double-parked delivery vans. She pushed through the side door of her building, because the revolving doors were locked on weekends. No one waited at the reception area, and only two guards stood by the security checkpoint. Lily took a deep breath, imagining herself in a relaxed yoga position, and smiled.

The guard looked at her identity card and then her face. "Good morning, Ms Aaron. Working on a Sunday?"

Lily peered at the guard's nameplate. "Good morning, Bill. Isn't that stupid? I left an important file on my desk."

"Yes, Ms. Aaron, sorry you had to come out on such a day."

"Thanks, Bill. It stopped raining at least, and the sun is trying to come out. Maybe I can get some shopping in since I'm uptown now. You have a nice day."

Lily realized she was holding her breath as she walked to the elevators. It came out in a whoosh of air, and she breathed in deeply through her nose. Inside the elevator, she sank against the wall so it could hold her up. She would definitely have fodder for her next book, a reality check on fear. Feeling silly, she pulled a pair of thin black leather gloves from her pocket and pulled them on.

What am I doing? her conscience asked.

Protecting yourself, now move it, self-preservation answered.

"All right, all right, don't push," Lily said aloud to the air. Then, feeling foolish, she pushed the button for her own floor. The Human Resources department was located on the floor above her office, but she didn't want anyone to see that she had gotten off the elevator at other than her own floor. Exiting the elevator, she headed for her own office and scooped up a manuscript, shoving it into a manila envelope so she would have something visible when she left the building. Then she took the stairs up one flight and opened the door to the reception area for Human Resources. Since it was the first place visitors saw, the area was furnished in minimalist modern, with soft gray leather sofas and chairs and glass and chrome tables. The only color came from oversized geometric paintings that immediately captured the eye.

Lily didn't see or sense any sign of life, and moved quietly toward the records room, a few doors down from the receptionist's desk. As she feared the door lock was a keypad, but she knew that the receptionist, Mary Ann Clark, hired for her blonde and bountiful beauty and not her brains, would have written down the numbers somewhere. Lily began on the top of the desk, flipping through the calendar and lifting each object to check underneath. Then she began pulling open the drawers, finding candy and more candy. Lily pictured the woman; how did she keep her figure? The next drawer was a jumble of Tampons, cosmetics, hairbrushes and mousse, a miniscule pair of thongs, and a package of strawberry-scented condoms.

Hmm! Her mind flitted to Ken and strawberries. *Stop it, Lily.* She felt around under each drawer and under the top of the desk. Finally, in the bottom drawer under a pile of fashion magazines, Lily found a small red leather book. She almost didn't look inside, thinking it was an address book. Nevertheless, Lily flipped through listings of the beauty salon, gym, Mom, Sis, girlfriends and men...lots and lots of men. *Busy bunny.* Lily mused.

There it was, listed as a phone number under the Ds next to the name, R. Door. Lily shook her head in wonder. Maybe the buxom blonde bunny wasn't as dumb as she appeared. Grabbing a sticky note and a pen, she copied the numbers, put the address book back in the drawer, and closed it. Looking around to make sure no one had suddenly appeared, she went to the door and punched in the numbers.

Her hand shook so hard that she had to key the numbers in twice before the door opened. "I am definitely not a role model character in one of my novels," Lily muttered to her pounding heart. She softly closed it behind her and moved to the file drawers. Thank goodness the company still kept paper files, because she wasn't a hacker and didn't know anything about accessing computer passwords. She opened the drawer marked "U to W," and there it was—"Warren, T." The file was thin, and Lily felt her stomach flop. She hoped this wasn't a complete waste of time. Lily looked around, hoping for a copy machine, and once again the gods smiled on her. It sat forlornly in a corner, just waiting to warm up. Lily turned it on and continued to read until the machine beeped once. Then she quickly copied the five pages in the file and turned off the machine. Returning the file to the drawer, she closed it and picked up the copied pages. Folding them and tucking them into her backpack, Lily opened the door and peered around...still empty.

A winking light caught her eye and she looked up at the elevator panel. A car was coming up, only three floors away. Heart pounding, she ran toward the stairway, then stopped short. The manuscript. She whirled around and raced back to the desk. Snatching up the manila envelope she had left on Mary Ann's desk, Lily just made it through the door to the stairwell when the elevator pinged and the doors slid open. She quietly pulled the door shut behind her, praying that whoever got off the elevator wouldn't see the movement.

Grateful for her rubber-soled shoes, Lily ran down the stairs to the second floor. Opening the stairwell door, Lily saw an empty hallway. Racing to the elevator, she pushed the button, muttering, "Please let it be empty." Holding her breath, Lily watched the doors open, and exhaled when no one appeared. She took the elevator down to the lobby so the guards would see her coming from her own floor, and waved the manila envelope at them. "Have a good day, guys." Vaguely, she wondered who had been visiting the fourth floor. Maybe there was another security guard checking each floor. Feeling like some scared heroine in one of her own novels, she jaywalked directly across the street.

Still shaky, Lily sank down on a chair in the virtually empty Java Cafe and sipped a decadent Cocoa Frappe with whipped cream and chocolate drizzle. She deserved it after her first and absolutely last criminal break-in. Slowly she savored the rich and very fattening chocolate cream concoction and sighed, picturing extra laps on the treadmill. *This little escapade had better be worth it.*

Her cell phone suddenly burst into song and she fumbled in her backpack before the call terminated into the "missed call" dungeon. Lily glanced at the name and smiled.

"Hi, Ken."

"What are you doing?"

"Indulging myself."

"Wasn't last night enough indulgence to last a while?"

"Mmmm! I'm greedy."

"How about dinner?"

"That depends on what's for dessert?"

"Hmmm, I'll have to think about that; something smooth, sweet, and satisfying."

Lily giggled. "Nice alliteration. You should have been a writer."

"I'd rather write on your back with my fingers dipped in chocolate, then—"

"Stop, stop."

"Oh alright, if you insist. You choose tonight's restaurant."

Lily gave him the name of a famous New York delicatessen in mid-town. "I'm in the mood for a thick pastrami sandwich."

"I'll pick you up at six o'clock."

"Yum!"

"Indeed!"

Lily clicked off the phone, her eyes glazed. Ken was definitely a charmer, and sexy as hell.

***

Five hours later, Lily and Ken sat close together in a circular booth. What once were plates of corned beef and pastrami sandwiches ringed by side dishes of cole slaw, pickles, and potato salad lay in shreds and crumbs on the table before them. Lily sipped her cream soda and sighed. "Food for the gods and goddesses."

"I'm sure all the cardiologists in New York are lined up to take our cholesterol counts."

Lily giggled, drunk from her favorite food. "I don't have that problem, do you?"

"It doesn't matter. I wouldn't have missed this in a heart attack."

"A man after my own heart."

"Oh, it's not your heart I want, Lily Aaron." His fingers tickled her thigh and worked their way up.

Her breathing grew rapid. Under the tablecloth Lily opened her thighs and Ken gently massaged her until she groaned. He leaned over and nuzzled her neck. Lily moved a few steps closer to out-of-control. A waiter appeared in her vision, and she closed her legs and pulled away. Placing his hand in his lap, Ken smiled up at the waiter. "We'll take the check now, please."

The waiter diplomatically ignored the change of position. "Of course, sir. Was everything to your satisfaction?"

Ken looked at her, and Lily said, "Absolutely fantastic, thank you."

As soon as Ken paid the bill, they went outside and hailed a taxi. Ken gave the driver the address and pulled Lily into his arms, kissing her deeply. Lily melted. She knew this was the night it would happen, and she was ready. They barely made it to her apartment. Shutting the door with his foot, Ken scooped her up and carried her into the bedroom. Their lovemaking was a frantic tangle of sweating bodies, until they both lay breathless in each other's arms.

Ken smoothed back Lily's hair and kissed her, slowly moving his tongue down her body. "Now we go slow," he murmured between her breasts.

Lily arched her back and moaned, winding her fingers into his curls.

Fran Orenstein

Chapter 13

All appeared peaceful at work. Nobody said anything about an intruder and the security checkpoint seemed calm. Tory caught up to her at the elevator. "So?"

"You are relentless, Tory."

"You did it!"

Lily glanced at the people standing near them. "Hush! I'm not discussing it in the lobby with a crowd around us."

"Okay, sorry; noon in the cafeteria."

"Deal."

Alison had taken the morning off for a dental appointment, so Lily didn't have to deal with her questions, too. She picked up the first manuscript, trying not to think about yesterday's escapade, or last night's for that matter. Every time the elevator pinged, she expected security to appear at her door. She told herself she was being ridiculous. Every so often she found herself thinking about Ken. She reread so many paragraphs that she finally gave up and turned to the email.

She was grateful when the clock finally called a halt to the painful effort of working. This was an impossible situation; she would have to get some control over her nerves and libido. Now, though she had Tory to deal with, and then Alison would be back at one o'clock. Oh, God, why did everything happen at once?

Lily stood in the doorway of the cafeteria searching for Tory, while at the same time looking for Ted Warren. She didn't see him at a table or at the service counter. This was ridiculous…she couldn't go on hiding from him. What could he possibly do in such a public place? There must have been sixty or seventy people there.

Tory waved from a table in the back of the room. Lily nodded and grabbed a tray. She barely noticed the food, tossing a sandwich, drink, and apple on the tray and getting in line at the checkout. Sliding into a seat, she said. "He isn't here."

"Who?"

"Ted," she whispered. "Please keep your voice down."

Tory looked around. "Uh, sure, but why? Are you hiding something?"

Lily shook her head. "Of course not, I just don't want the world to know."

"I think it's kind of exciting."

"He's stalking me, and that's not exciting. In fact, stalkers kill people."

"I don't think Ted could kill a fly. He probably just has a crush on you."

"Then why does he keep calling me Laurel?"

"Maybe he's just absentminded."

"Or he's fixated on someone from his past named Laurel who looks like me. That's what serial killers do, they fixate on people who remind them of somebody who wronged them. Then something triggers them, and they start to kill women who look like her."

Tory laughed. "I think you're blowing this all out of proportion; too many nights writing mysteries and watching all those crime shows on television."

Lily paused and then laughed. "You're right, I'm sounding paranoid." She leaned closer, lowering her voice so Tory could barely hear her. "If my body is found hacked to shreds, you'll know who did it."

Tory managed to keep a straight face. "Absolutely! What's the expression? 'I'll finger Ted Warren'."

They chewed for a few minutes, then Tory said, "So tell me about Mr. Gorgeous."

"He's fun to be with, sexy as hell, and I like him a lot."

"I'm jealous."

"Why, what happened to the actuary?"

Tory shrugged. "He took up with a salsa dancer he met at his cousin's wedding."

"You're kidding, right?"

"I wish I were."

"How did you find out?"

"He told me."

"What?" Lily clapped her hand over her mouth when several people at nearby tables looked around.

"We went to a bar. He had too many beers and he called me Delores. So I asked him who Delores was and he grinned at me and said, 'Ooops'."

"Ooops? He must have said something else."

"Oh, yeah, he told me she had long black hair and blazing black eyes, and could really shake her booty. And, he went home with her, an all-nighter."

Lily rolled her eyes. "Oh my God, I'm so sorry. He must have been pretty drunk or really stupid, telling you all that. So, what did you do?"

Tory blinked and grinned. "I was nice. I didn't smash a bottle of beer on his head. Instead, I tipped my glass of beer in his lap, called him a few choice names, and walked out."

"Always the lady." Lily grinned. "You are amazing, Tory."

"Waste of good beer."

Lily laughed so hard she nearly choked. That resulted in hiccups, which set them both off. "I give up," Lily said when she could breathe again. "I'm going back upstairs. Are you all right?"

"I'll be fine. I'm just glad I found out before introducing him to my family."

"Somebody will come along, Tory."

"He'd better; clock's a-ticking. I hope Ken works out for you. Go slow, though."

"I'm trying."

They rode back up in the elevator with the returning lunch crowd. Lily felt relieved that Ted

Warren was missing in action. She had too many things going at once, and didn't need his distracting behavior. Maybe she was reading too much into it. He had probably confused her with someone else, or he kept mistaking her name. Tonight she would go through his personnel file.

Alison called in sick the rest of the day, mumbling on the phone. Apparently, the dental work was more than she could handle, and she needed to lie down and take a painkiller. Lily commiserated with her, but felt relieved that she didn't have to contend with her other mother's questions, too. Lily felt guilty, since Alison only had her best interests at heart, but there was only so much room in her brain to process everything that was happening.

She closed and locked her office door and pulled her yoga mat out of a file drawer. Happy she had worn loose slacks, Lily assumed a yoga position, emptying her brain of everything and concentrating on a serene lake, surrounded by a wildflower meadow. Whenever thoughts of Ted Warren or Ken intruded, she pushed them away and focused on the soothing water. After ten minutes she rose, feeling refreshed and calm. The rest of the afternoon passed without incident, and by the end of the day, Lily felt she had accomplished a lot. She went home in a happy mood, not worrying about anyone following her, thinking of Ken Braun.

***

After dinner, Lily tried to concentrate on Ted Warren's personnel file, but relentless images of the previous night intruded. She wondered if Ken had any flaws. He seemed the perfect man; smart, educated, a good listener, incredibly handsome, and a fantastic lover. It was almost too good to be true, but Lily hadn't detected anything negative, and by age thirty-three, her antenna was on high alert. Could a serious relationship really develop? It would be very easy to dive into those green eyes and fall in love. Why hadn't anyone scooped him up already? *Stop*, she admonished herself, *don't get picky again, he might just be the real thing. Give it a chance.*

Lily pushed thoughts of Ken away and looked down at the words on the paper. She read Ted's application and wondered if anything on the paper was true. He had graduated from a small college in Connecticut at twenty-six. Had he gone at night, accounting for the fact that he was an older graduate, or had he done something else between high school and college? There was nothing on the application accounting for those years. She didn't even know where he had lived as a child, or the name of his high school. Was it in Connecticut or elsewhere?

After college, Ted had worked in the computer division at a small insurance company in Hartford, a no-brainer since it was the insurance capital of the east coast. Human Resources would have checked his references, or reference in the singular, so he must have worked there. Then how did he end up at a large publishing house in New York?

The only emergency contact he entered was his sister, and Lily had already checked her name on the computer, again coming up with no information. It was as though they had slid out from under a rock, or emerged fully-grown from a seed. According to the application, they lived in Brooklyn, so he probably took the subway to work every day. What difference did that make? There were more questions than answers.

His boss said he was a solid worker, always on time, just not sociable. Lily imagined he was probably someone who melted into the office furniture, following directions and never making waves. People like Ted didn't rise far, but then every company needed the worker bees who were content to do their assigned job and nothing more. Maybe he even enjoyed it. He had just passed his probationary period, so there wasn't much else. Lily realized she had taken a foolish chance to get very little information. She shredded the evaluation and folded the application, tucking it into the deepest compartment of her backpack.

Lily yawned. Should she go any further with this?

The phone rang. Lily glanced at the name and sank down on the bed, stretching, a cat-like smile on her face. "Hello, Ken."

His silky voice oozed from the telephone speaker. "Know what I'm thinking right now?"

"Why don't you tell me?" Lily purred. For the next ten minutes she listened to Ken describe, in minute detail, what he would like to do to her, leaving Lily shivering in sexual frustration. "You are so naughty, torturing me like this."

"Yum! You taste delicious. Good-night, Tiger Lily."

Lily pouted as she hung up the phone.

Fran Orenstein

***

Ten miles away, Ken Braun licked his lips and rolled over on the red satin sheets, continuing in real-time the exploration he had been describing on the phone.

CHAPTER 14

The week ended with no Ted Warren sighting. On Friday afternoon, Lily and Tory left the building together.

"Thank goodness Ted Warren didn't try to corner me this week," Lily said.

"I haven't seen him around."

"Hopefully that last encounter scared him enough to change his habits. There are over a thousand employees in this building; there doesn't have to be a reason to pay attention to him at all. If he hadn't come over that day in the cafeteria, calling me Laurel, I would never have even noticed him. Well, maybe I would have smelled him if we were on the same elevator."

Tory giggled. "Maybe he's on vacation."

"Maybe he quit."

"I like that scenario better. Changing the subject, are you seeing Ken this weekend?"

"He's coming over tonight."

"Whoo, hoo!"

"Stop it. He got tickets for an off-Broadway show for tomorrow night. It's a surprise, so I can't even tell you the name of the play."

"The man is full of surprises."

"He does keep the relationship interesting."

"I'll bet. Do you think he has any brothers or cousins or friends?"

Lily laughed. "I'll ask him. Maybe I can set up a blind date."

Tory groaned. "I hate blind dates."

"Then, you should start drinking lattes at Java Cafe."

They hugged, giggling like tenth graders. "Whoops, there's my bus." Tory raced to the bus stop, while Lily walked to the subway entrance.

***

She never saw the woman standing in the doorway across the street, watching Lily descend the stairs. Once Lily disappeared from sight, the woman turned and walked in the other direction, flipping open a cell phone.

***

Sunday morning, Lily sat cross-legged on the mat, hands on her thighs, thumb and forefinger forming a circle. Her serene face appeared almost childlike, framed by her untamed, curly blond hair. A loose sweat suit tried to camouflage the lush curves of her petite body, failing miserably. Carlos Nakai flute music flowed from the stereo. Lily tried to empty her mind, but last night intruded. Ken certainly knew how to make love to a woman and leave her wanting more.

Once more putting the memories of his hands and lips aside, Lily breathed slowly and deeply three times, imagining a serene lake in a lush green meadow. Sinking into the meditation, her shoulders relaxed.

She jerked at the harsh sound of the door buzzer.

"So much for serenity," she grumbled.

Rising gracefully, she reached over to turn off the music. The buzzer sounded again.

"Alright, I'm coming," she called. "Just stop buzzing."

Peering through the peephole, she saw a man and a woman. The man held up a police badge with a gold shield. *Now what?*

She opened the door as far as the double chains and looked out. "Can I help you?"

"Lily Aaron?" the man said.

"What do you want?" she asked, unwilling to acknowledge her name.

"Are you Lily Aaron?" he said louder.

"And I'm asking you what you want," she said.

"Ma'am, I'm Detective Roy Jamison and this is my partner, Detective Ann Dyson. Can we please come in and talk to you?"

Lily reached for the pad and pencil she kept on the small table by the door. "Let me see your badges again?" Lily asked.

The detectives sighed and held up the badges. Lily wrote down the badge numbers and names. "Are you from the local precinct?"

"Ma'am...." Jamison started, annoyed.

Dyson interrupted, glaring at her partner. "Excuse me, Ms. Aaron. You're absolutely right to be cautious. Please just call 911 and ask for the Downtown-East precinct. They'll vouch for us."

"Yes, well, big bad city," Lily muttered as she shut and locked the door. She called the police station and verified that Dyson and Jamison were who they claimed to be. Then she opened the door. "So, again, what do you want?"

The officers came in and sat down in the chairs Lily pointed to. "Ms. Aaron, do you know someone named Ted Warren?" Jamison asked.

Lily looked at them carefully before she nodded. "We work in the same company. Why? Has something happened to him?"

"Why? Do you think something happened to him?" Jamison countered.

Lily shrugged. "It just seemed weird that you would be coming to my house to ask me about him."

"When did you last see him?" Dyson asked.

"I really don't remember. Maybe last week some time. You haven't answered my question. Has something happened to him?"

The officers looked at each other. "He was found dead in his apartment yesterday morning."

Lily sucked in her breath and paled. "Oh my God. What happened? Did he have a heart attack?" She was babbling. Lily pressed her lips together. Her forehead wrinkled. "Wait a minute...since when does the police inform a virtual stranger that somebody died? I mean, we worked for the same company, but I didn't really know him. And why me? There must be over three hundred people at the office, and over a thousand in the building. Are you talking to all of them? What's going on?"

"Ma'am, we'd like to ask the questions," Jamison said.

Lily pursed her lips. She knew enough from her research and writing mystery novels to get a sense of the scene. "I'm sure you would. I'm also sure there's more to this than you're willing to say, so not being stupid, I'm calling an attorney friend of mine." She went into the kitchen, leaving the two officers rolling their eyes, and called Ken.

Lily returned in a few minutes with a bottle of water and sat down. She thought briefly about offering them a beverage, but decided she didn't feel hospitable. In fact, she was just plain annoyed and not a little worried.

The three of them awkwardly stared into space in silence for twenty minutes, carefully avoiding eye contact, until the buzzer sounded. Lily opened the door and Ken Braun entered. The weathered briefcase seemed out of place with his jeans and white shirt, but a sport jacket gestured to his profession.

"My attorney, Kenneth Braun."

"Detectives Roy Jamison and Ann Dyson." Jamison offered his hand.

Ken nodded and reluctantly shook hands. "Lily told me you're questioning her about someone at work who died? It seems to me that this isn't routine. Suppose you tell me the reason."

"Ms. Aaron is making more of a fuss than necessary. We're just trying to find out where she was last Friday night," Jamison said.

"And why would you be interested in her whereabouts?" Ken asked.

"One of her co-workers was found dead in his apartment," Dyson answered.

"And...?" Ken said.

"Well, it wasn't a natural death," Dyson said.

Lily gasped and covered her mouth. Ken reached out and grasped her arm. He turned to her and shook his head.

"So he what? Committed suicide, was murdered?" Ken asked.

"It wasn't suicide," Dyson said. Jamison sent her a warning look.

"And how does Lily factor into this?"

"Look, we can't tell you everything right now, but suffice it to say, she does," Jamison replied.

"You'll have to do better than that," Ken said. "In fact, I think this pointless discussion is over, unless you are prepared to arrest her for some mysterious crime, or tell us more."

The officers stood. "You'll be hearing from us, Ms. Aaron. Stay in town," Jamison said.

Lily slammed the door on them and turned. "What's going on, Ken? I don't understand. I told you about his mistaking me for someone else. You know that I hardly knew the man. We didn't even work in the same area. He simply mistook me for someone else. My

God, the guy was a computer geek; I'm an editor. Do they think I did something to him?" Tears welled.

Ken pulled her close. "I don't know, Lily. I'll get my investigators on it first thing tomorrow. The cops must have some reason for coming here to question you. You were smart to call me and not tell them anything."

"I write mysteries, Ken. I would probably kill my heroine if she answered the cops' questions without an attorney."

Ken tilted his head and grinned. Lily sniffed and laughed. "I can't believe I just said that."

Ken laughed, too. "You think of your characters as real people. So it slipped your mind who taps the computer keys."

He took off his jacket, draped it over the back of the dining room chair, and sat down. Opening the briefcase, he pulled out a yellow legal pad and a pencil. Lily took a deep breath and sat down opposite him.

"Tomorrow first thing, I'll call Carol Bloom. She's a top defense attorney in our firm. Now let me ask some questions," Ken said.

"Wait a minute. You said this Carol Bloom is a defense attorney. Do you think I'm going to need one?"

"Relax, it's just a precaution. Maybe somebody told the police Ted might be stalking you."

"Who would have done that? Only Alison and Tory knew, and I trust them completely." Lily looked up. "And you; you knew too, Ken."

"Look at me, Lily. I wouldn't hurt you for the world."

Lily heard Ken's soothing voice and floated into his green eyes.

"That's better. Now, since we don't know the time of death, just tell me what you did last Friday."

Lily saw the twinkle in his eye and capitulated to his charm. "Let's see. I worked all day, and that night I had drinks with a very sexy, handsome man; after which, we satisfied our starving libidos until the wee hours of Saturday morning. We slept in—"

"Among other things."

"Right. After a late breakfast—"

"And other things." Ken grinned.

Lily rolled her eyes. "We drove to the shore. We ate an early dinner at a fantastic seafood restaurant, probably ate too many oysters, and came back for a repeat performance of libidinous high jinks that definitely transcended Friday night. Afterward, he took me to see an off-Broadway play and came back here for more...well, you know. An early morning run, breakfast and...then I threw him out so I could meditate. Enter the cops."

Ken cleared his throat. "Um, let me think about this." He looked up and grinned. "Last night really transcended Friday night?"

Lily moved around the table and squirmed onto Ken's lap. "Absolutely!"

"Stop squirming, vixen. I'm trying to take notes," Ken laughed.

"Note this." Lily patted the bump in his jeans.

"All right, you asked for it." Ken picked her up and carried her to the bedroom.

An hour later, Lily stretched and arched her back. She rubbed Ken's thigh with her foot.

He leaned on one elbow and stared at her naked body, a sly grin on his face.

"You remind me of the Cheshire Cat," Lily purred.

He licked his lips. "Mmm! You must be the cream." He leaned over her, but Lily rolled out from under his body and rolled off the bed.

"I need a shower and then—"

"I'll join you." Ken sat up and swung his feet off the bed.

"Oh, no! Then we'll never get back to my problem. This was just a break."

Ken moaned and fell back on the bed. Lily looked at him and smiled. "Always at the ready, aren't you?"

"Like a soldier at arms," he quipped.

Lily shook her head. "Well, at ease soldier! I'll be right out."

***

Ken watched her gather fresh clothes and enter the bathroom, closing the door behind her. The lock clicked. As soon as he heard the shower, he reached over and grabbed his cell phone. He pressed speed dial and waited for several rings until it was picked up.

"She's in the shower and can't hear a thing. It's working perfectly." He listened and then said, "You know better than that. I'll see you later." He ended the call and pulled on his clothes. He would wait to shower until later, when he would certainly need it again, anyway.

***

Lily was tying back her wet hair as she came into the kitchen. Ken sat at the table, the legal pad and pen ready. Ken asked her about her relationship with Ted Warren.

"What relationship? This is ridiculous. You know all this. I barely knew the man except to nod in passing, and not even that much. I told you, he worked in the computer department, I work in editorial. If it weren't for his obsession with my name, we would have had nothing to do with each other." Lily ran out of breath.

"All right Tiger Lily, calm down. If the cops are serious, they're going to ask you the same question."

"Well, I can only tell them what I just told you. I didn't know him!"

"Take it easy, Lily. I'm not the enemy."

Lily put her head in her hands. "I'm sorry, Ken. This is really making me nervous. I don't understand what they want from me."

Ken stood up and walked behind her. He kneaded her shoulders and pulled her back against him. "They must have found some connection."

"What could they possibly find? I barely knew the guy."

"Let's hope the cops don't come back, and they find someone else to focus on.

Meanwhile, tell me everything you know about this guy." He slid his hands down her chest.

Lily jerked away from him. "I told you, I don't know anything."

Ken persisted. "You'd be surprised what you know. For instance, what did he look like?"

"A geek, sloppy, like that kid in the Peanuts cartoons. Always had some stain down the front of his shirt. His hair never looked like it was combed, and he smelled like sour milk and unwashed clothes. He didn't socialize. Came in, worked, ate lunch alone, and went wherever."

"So you didn't like him," Ken said.

"I didn't like or dislike him. I didn't know him. I don't even know if he had ever been married or had kids or a cat. He had a sister who came to the holiday party, and he read the Bible. He was part of the furniture, you know what I mean?" Lily said, thinking about the stolen personnel file. She would have to destroy the application as soon as Ken left. Then she wondered why she kept the information to herself. Ken's voice distracted her.

"A non-entity."

Lily nodded. "A non-entity," she repeated. "Good term for him. He disappeared into the surroundings.

"Anything else?" Ken watched her, forehead wrinkled in concentration. She must have sensed him, because she looked up at him with cow-eyes, brown and gentle.

"What?"

"Nothing," Ken said, retrieving the pencil.

"No, no, you were looking at me for a reason."

"I like to look at you, Lily." He reached across and grasped her hand gently. He rubbed his thumb around her palm.

It tingled. Lily pulled back. "If you keep doing that, we'll be back in bed again."

Ken shrugged. "So?"

"So, that won't help if I'm in jail for something I didn't do. Get professional." "Right. Okay, moving on. Do you know where he lives?" Ken asked, withdrawing his hand.

Lily lied. "Not a clue."

Ken put the pad and pencil back in his briefcase and clicked it shut. "I can't do any more until I find out what's going on. So what do you want to do now?" He smirked.

"Eat," Lily said.

"That wasn't exactly what I had in mind."

"I know just what you had in mind, but I'm hungry. Here, call out for Chinese." She handed him a well-worn menu. "I'm going to dry my hair."

"Need help?"

Lily shook her head. "Nope! Just feed me."

Ken stood up.

"With egg drop soup and shrimp fried rice," she said, pointedly looking at his crotch.

Ken laughed. "You sure know how to torture a guy, Tiger Lily."

She flounced out of the room, hips swaying, wiggling her rear end.

Later that night, Lily shredded Ted's employment application and sighed in relief. She wasn't cut out for this spying. "Leave it to the characters in your books," she mumbled.

Chapter 15

Monday morning at seven, Lily called Ken. "I don't know what to do, Ken. Should I go to work or not?" Lily wailed into the phone.

"Just go about your business today as you would ordinarily do. Go to work. Everybody is going to be talking about what happened. You'll probably know more than I do by 9:05."

"Hmmm. I guess so. What if the cops come around again asking questions?"

"Just don't answer. Don't say anything to anybody. Ask questions, but don't volunteer any information, understand?" Ken advised. "I'm going to talk to Carol as soon as I get in."

"Right, zip my lip."

"Good, and keep it zipped," Ken said. "One-way gossip—"

"Incoming only," Lily said.

"Smart lady," Ken responded. "I don't have court today, so call me anytime. I'll make sure everyone knows to put you through. And…don't say it. I'll keep my cell phone on and next to me."

"You'd better."

Lily got dressed and went to work.

She got as far as the lobby of the building. Scattered groups of agitated people milled around, talking.

"Oh, Lily, did you hear?" Alison rushed over and grabbed her arm. She continued before Lily could say anything. "It's just awful. Ted Warren is dead. They say he was murdered over the weekend. His sister found him. They think he was shot or stabbed or something."

Lily feigned shock. "My God, that's awful. Do they know who did it?"

Ali shook her head. "The cops are upstairs now, going through his office. They brought in some computer guy to check his emails and stuff."

Lily nodded. Out of the corner of her eye she saw Tory pushing through the crowd.

"Did you hear? It's just terrible, that poor man. Well, not that anybody liked him, but he was still a human being."

Lily nodded again. "Awful!"

"Could have been anyone, even someone he knew, right Lily?" Tory suggested.

Lily retorted angrily, "What are you suggesting?"

Tory shrugged and looked at her strangely. "I didn't mean anything, Lily."

Ali spoke up. "Both of you, calm down. We're all just nervous, that's all. It's not like it's something that happens every day."

"Well, Lily can't say that, right?" Tory said.

"What?" Lily rounded on Tory.

"Hey, I just meant that he was stalking you, you know what I mean," Tory said, backing off.

"Oh," Lily said, "Speaking of stalking, did you say anything about Ted and me to anyone?"

"Hey, I'm your friend, remember?"

Lily looked at her. "That's not an answer, Tory."

Alison jumped into the budding argument, "We're all upset. I didn't say anything and I'm sure Tory didn't either. Let's just keep things between us, okay?"

Just then the elevator doors opened and Detectives Jamison and Dyson appeared. Six uniformed officers followed them, carrying boxes and computers.

"What are they doing?" Ali asked. "They have two computers and a lot of boxes."

"Taking stuff from his office to look for clues, I guess," Tory answered. "Right, Lily?"

Lily nodded, unable to speak. Could she trust Tory? She ducked behind them, praying that neither of the detectives would spot her in the crowd. She held her breath until they left the lobby and everyone filed toward the elevators.

Lily was afraid that one of the computers was hers. What else might they have taken from her office? An unfinished manuscript she was rewriting? There wasn't anything incriminating. She had nothing to hide. So why was she so scared? Suddenly, she desperately had to go to the bathroom.

"Listen, I'll be right up. I need the little girls' room," she whispered to Ali. Lily pushed her way through the crowd to the far side of the lobby, where the public rest rooms were located. Once inside, she quickly used the toilet, washed her hands, and punched in Ken's cell phone. He answered on the first ring, thank God.

"I'm so scared," Lily said. "I think they were in my office. I'm afraid to go upstairs."

"Calm down, honey. Where are you?"

"In the public restroom in the lobby. They kept everybody downstairs. The cops just left, they didn't see me. They were carrying two computers and far more boxes than one office would fill."

Ken drew a breath. "Okay. Go upstairs and into your office. Act shocked if you find it's been searched. They had to have a warrant, and it had to state a reason. Talk to your boss. Innocently ask him what's going on."

"But won't he already know the cops are interested in me if they searched my office and confiscated my computer?" Lily asked.

"That's okay. You don't have to tell him anything. Let him tell you. Remember, information is power," Ken said.

Lily nodded, than realized Ken couldn't see her. "Just leave your cell phone on, all right?"

"Absolutely! Remember, Kenneth Braun, Attorney for the downtrodden and innocent, is on the job."

Lily laughed in spite of her fear. "That's why I love you, Ken Braun, Attorney for the pitiful and weak."

"Ha! Tiger Lily, pitiful and weak? I don't think so." Click.

She smiled and closed her eyes, wishing it would all go away. Then she put away the cell phone and walked out of the restroom. The last stragglers were entering the elevators as she crossed the lobby and joined them.

The second floor was chaos. Nobody was working. As she exited the elevator, there was sudden silence. Everyone turned and looked at her. Lily saw Ali frantically waving. Lily took a deep breath and plunged into the fray. The crowd parted like the Red Sea, then the cacophony started again. She ignored the voices and hands that reached out, heading straight for Ali, who was motioning toward Lily's office.

Ali grabbed her arm and practically manhandled her inside. The office was a mess. The first thing she noticed was the missing computer. Thank goodness she had her laptop at home, and all her own books and manuscripts were backed up and stored at her parent's house. The once orderly stacks of manuscripts and papers were strewn all over the surface.

"What the hell...?" Lily was dumfounded. Even knowing the police had probably been in her office, she hadn't expected it to be this bad. "Where's the computer?"

"Oh, Lily, those awful cops, they just came barreling in here with George from personnel and shut the door. Then they came out with three boxes and your computer. They didn't go into anybody else's office, just yours, and I guess poor Ted's." Ali clutched her throat, gasping. She fumbled at her pocket for her inhaler, then closed her lips over the opening and pressed.

"Here, sit down. Breathe, Ali." Lily pulled out her chair and lowered Ali into it. "Just relax and breathe," Lily said, rubbing the back of her secretary's neck. "You don't want to have a full-blown asthma attack." She continued to rub Ali's neck, speaking soothingly to her, until Ali could breathe again.

"That's better," Lily said.

"But—" Ali started to say.

"But, nothing. Don't you worry about anything. It's my problem, and I'm going to find out what's going on," Lily said.

At that moment, the phone rang. Lily put her hand on Ali's shoulder when she tried to reach for the receiver. "Let me get it, you just sit there and relax."

Lily picked up the phone. "Lily Aaron."

"Ms. Aaron, Mr. Wilde would like to see you in his office," his secretary said, formally. *Uh oh, trouble.* Dorrie always called her Lily.

Lily said, "On my way." She slumped and tried to focus. This would have to be the biggest lie of all. She didn't know if she could pull it off. Then she thought of the stakes and straightened her back.

Lily helped Ali from the chair. "Why don't you take a break? If you don't feel well, just go home. It doesn't look like I'm getting much done today, anyway."

"I'll be fine. I just need some fresh air. Maybe I'll get a muffin and tea. I'll stay, though. I can clean up the office, Lily."

"Just be sure you're okay. The office isn't going anywhere," Lily said, thinking, *but maybe I am.*

Lily took the elevator to the fifth floor executive offices. John Wilde, her immediate boss, was the managing editor. They had a good working relationship and he was a decent guy...she hoped.

"I'm here, Dorrie," Lily said.

Dorrie looked at her strangely and tried to keep a distance between them as she knocked on her boss's door. When he said come in, she opened the door and then moved quickly out of the way behind her desk.

She's afraid of me. Maybe she thinks murder is catching. Lily walked into John's office. He wasn't alone. Her two least favorite detectives were leaning against the wall. *I can do this,* Lily thought. "Good morning, John," she said, ignoring the detectives.

"Uh, good morning, Lily. Uh, I believe you already know Detectives Jamison and Dyson." John's eyes pleaded with her to forgive him for the ambush.

Lily ignored him. Turning to the detectives, she said, "I see you wrecked my office this morning." Lily was hoping they would give something away.

Jamison shrugged. "Just doing our job, Ms. Aaron."

"Really? Harassing innocent people, terrorizing my secretary into an asthma attack, destroying company property...quite a job. I'm sure you must enjoy it."

John looked stricken. "Is Alison alright?"

"She will be. I've instructed her to take a long break and go home if she doesn't feel better. That is, if we don't have to take her to the hospital." Lily glared at the detectives. Dyson squirmed, but Jamison didn't seem bothered at all.

"We have some more questions for you, Ms. Aaron," Jamison said.

Lily flipped open her cell phone and speed dialed. At the connection she said, "Ken, I've been ambushed by two cops in my boss's office."

She listened for a moment. "More questions."

Again she listened. "They wrecked my office, took the computer and files. Ali had an asthma attack. John's secretary is afraid of me."

More listening. "Right."

She looked up at the detectives. "My attorney's on the way." She sat down in a chair and crossed her legs.

"You mean your boyfriend, don't you?" Jamison said.

Lily reddened, but locked her jaw and refused to rise to his bait.

A few minutes of uncomfortable silence followed and John stood up. "I think we should move to the conference room since Ms. Aaron's attorney will be joining us."

He didn't wait for an answer, but left his office, the detectives and Lily following him. "Dorrie, call down to two, please, and find out where Alison Pierce is right now. Apparently, she got so upset by the police search of Ms. Aaron's office that she had an asthma attack. I want to make sure she's okay." He glared pointedly at the detectives. Dyson had the decency to look down at her shoes. Jamison glared back.

"Yes, sir, of course. I'll see to it right away." Dorrie sent Lily a nasty look, as if it were entirely her fault. Lily shrugged. Win, lose, lose, win. Maybe she should be pulling daisy petals.

"Oh, and please, some coffee for everybody. Thank you, Dorrie," John said.

Another nasty glance in her direction. Lily looked away.

They trailed behind John Wilde to the conference room. Ten minutes later the coffee arrived, with muffins. Lily was grateful for the coffee, but knew her throat would close over a dry muffin. That didn't stop Jamison and Dyson from stuffing their faces. Lily noted that at least John ignored his. He kept sneaking looks in her direction, apparently unsure of what was going on.

After another twenty minutes Ken arrived, with a woman Lily supposed was the firm's top defense attorney, Carol Bloom. *Thank God*! Lily thought, *score one for Ken.*

***

Detective Jamison groaned. Only Dyson heard and looked at Jamison, her eyebrows raised. Jamison shrugged and shook his head. *Shit*, he thought, *it would be Bloom*. Looking like a cookie-baking housewife and mother, with short, curly brown hair and innocent blue eyes, Carol smirked at the detective, as if she knew just what he was thinking. Behind her back, prosecutors referred to her as "The Barracuda," which Jamison thought she secretly relished. She had lost only one case in the past ten years, and then only because the client saw Jesus standing next to the judge, and he immediately fell to his knees and confessed.

***

Ken made the introductions and sat next to Lily. She was grateful for his support and foresight in bringing Carol. That move would block the cops before they could go the boyfriend route.

"Now then, I've been briefed and am now the attorney of record for Ms. Aaron. I would like to speak with my client before we have any discussion," Carol announced.

The police detectives sighed and followed John Wilde out of the room.

"Do you want me to represent you?" Carol asked.

Lily nodded.

"Fine, we can take care of the legal stuff later. Now, have you said anything to them?" she asked.

"Not a word. Ken warned me," Lily said.

"Wonderful, bring me up to date."

Lily told her about the weekend, keeping it neat and clean. She explained the cops visit to her apartment and Ken's part in it. Then she described her office, her secretary's reaction, and brought Carol up to date on this current meeting.

Carol looked hard at Lily. "Fine! Now I'm going to ask you a question, and if you prefer that Ken leave, then say so, but I need a true answer. Did you know the dead man other than as a co-worker?"

Lily jumped up. "Absolutely not! I didn't even know him as a co-worker. I don't know anything about him."

Ken pulled her down, back into her chair. "Take it easy, honey, she has to ask these questions."

Carol reached across and took Lily's hand. "I needed to ask you, Lily. Now when the police come back in, I want you to be calm. No outbursts. Understand?"

Lily nodded. "I'm sorry. I feel like nobody believes me besides Ken, but then I was with him the whole weekend."

"So he confirmed. I'm going to get them back in here. Relax, I'll handle it." Carol went to the door and called them in. She politely asked John Wilde if he would wait in his office until they were finished. Wilde glanced at Lily and left, pulling the door shut behind him.

"Why don't you tell me what is going on?" Carol asked the detectives when everyone was seated.

Jamison cleared his throat.

Lily thought, *I hope he chokes on that frog.*

"Ms. Aaron is a person of interest in the murder of one Theodore Warren," Jamison said.

Lily stiffened and Carol nudged her under the table. "I see," Carol said. "And in what way is she a person of interest?"

Jamison again cleared his throat, trying to get the words out. It was apparent that he didn't want to give out any information.

"Come on now, detective. You had a warrant to search Ms. Aaron's office and confiscate her computer and whatever else you took, so what was stated on the warrant?"

Dyson finally spoke up. "We believe Ms. Aaron was in Mr. Warren's apartment at the time of the murder."

Lily gasped. "What? That's not possible!"

Ken squeezed her arm. "Lily, don't say anything." Jamison growled. Dyson ignored him. "We just want to ask her some questions about her activities during the time of death."

"We don't know the time of death, or anything else about this alleged death. So why don't you fill us in, Detective Dyson?" Carol said, poising her pen over the pad.

"Ted Warren was found in his apartment on Saturday morning by his sister, who came to pick him up to go to a church event. He had been shot twice. Time of death was between midnight and 3:00 a.m. on Saturday morning," Dyson said.

"And what does this have to do with my client?" Carol asked.

Dyson looked at Jamison, who shrugged. She turned back to the attorney. "She was seen leaving the victim's building around the time of the murder."

Lily's jaw dropped. Ken's hand tightened on her arm. She was too stunned to react. How could this be possible? She was in bed with Ken, and he knew it, too. What the hell was happening?

"A witness?" Carol stated.

Jamison said, "Not exactly."

"Come on, detective, stop playing games. Was there a witness or not?"

"She was caught on the security camera in the lobby of the building at 2:15 a.m."

Carol turned to Lily, who shrugged. "My client has an alibi, detective."

Jamison ignored her. "We sent the photo through all the databases and came up with a close match in one of them."

"Which database?" Carol asked.

"The FBI database," Dyson said.

"What?" Lily croaked.

Ken leaned over and whispered, "Shhh. Let them talk."

Carol glanced at Lily. "The photo matched my client?"

"We don't have any doubt that it's Lily Aaron, Ms. Bloom," Dyson said, pulling an FBI wanted poster out of the file.

Carol looked at the poster and passed it to Ken and Lily. "This is not her name, detective, and the resemblance is sketchy at best."

"Well, it was probably an alias, or this is an alias; we have yet to determine which. The name was Laurel James, but it was Ms. Aaron's picture," Jamison said.

Lily jerked at the name, but Carol put her hand on Lily's arm. "What crime did she allegedly commit?"

It was Dyson's turn to hesitate. "Bank robbery. She drove the getaway car. There was a security camera, and she was also spotted outside the bank by a passerby. That's how they got the artist's sketch, which was close enough to the security photo to make a match."

Lily gasped. "What? That's impossible!"

Carol turned to Lily. "Be quiet, please." She turned back to the detectives, "When and where did this happen?"

Jamison consulted his notes. "March 22, 1995, in Mountain City, New Mexico."

Carol turned to Lily. "Do you recall where you were then?"

Lily frowned, concentrating. She'd never heard of Mountain City, New Mexico. She was so nervous she couldn't think, let alone remember where she was thirteen years ago. Ken squeezed her hand. Of course! "I was in college in Boston."

Jamison groaned. She had been over sixteen hundred miles away. "We'll have to verify your whereabouts, of course. Anybody you can think of who will be able to do that?"

Lily relaxed. "Everybody at my parent's twenty-fifth wedding anniversary party in Concord, Mass."

Jamison grumbled something, but Dyson seemed impressed. "We'll need names, of course."

"Fine," Lily said.

Jamison seemed puzzled. "So how do you account for the likeness to the drawing?"

"What kind of question is that? Witnesses are notoriously mistaken, and that photo is blurred."

"Okay, maybe the witness was wrong back then, but what about your picture on the security camera two nights ago?" Jamison persisted.

"Well, it must be a doppelganger," Lily said between clenched teeth.

"Let us be serious, this was not a ghost. Do you have a sister?" Dyson said.

Lily groaned. "No, I don't have sister or a brother." Then she muttered softly, "At least, not that I know of."

"How could you not know?" Jamison asked.

"I'm adopted," Lily whispered.

"What? I didn't hear that." Jamison raised his voice.

"You heard her perfectly, detective," Carol interjected. "Lily, don't say another word. Let me handle this. Obviously, there's been a mistake."

"Not on our account. She still hasn't told us where she was Friday night and Saturday morning," Jamison said.

"She was with me, or I was with her at her apartment," Ken said. "We spent the entire weekend together from 5:00 p.m. Friday until just before noon on Sunday. Then you were with her. Remember that?"

"Right...." Jamison asked. "You slept over, Mr. Braun?"

Ken nodded.

"And do you sleep soundly?"

"What are you getting at?" Ken said.

"She might have done anything while you were sleeping soundly, that's all." Jamison shrugged.

"That's ridiculous, Detective Jamison. You're grasping," Carol said.

Jamison stood up. "We'll follow up on that. Okay, we're done here for now. As I said before, don't leave the city, Ms. Aaron. We'll be in touch."

When they had left, Carol turned to Lily. "Come to my office as soon as possible, and we'll officially establish our attorney/client relationship. Ken, are you coming back to the office?"

"You go on back, Carol. Just give me a minute here."

Carol Bloom nodded and closed the door behind her. Ken turned to Lily. "Listen, this is just a misunderstanding. You were with me and you have a solid alibi." He put his arms around her and held her. Lily pressed her face into his jacket, trying to hold back the tears that threatened. Ken eased her back, holding her shoulders. "It's going to be fine, I promise. You'll be able to turn this into your best mystery novel when it's all over."

Lily attempted a bleak smile and nodded. "Thanks, Ken, for being here for me."

"You're special to me, Tiger Lily." He kissed her.

Lily forced a smile and sank into a chair.

***

Ken turned his back and smiled, softly closing the conference room door behind him. As soon as he exited the building, he flipped open his cell phone and punched a number. "It's going just as planned." He listened for a moment and whispered, "Sounds delectable, see you tonight."

***

John Wilde returned and politely suggested that Lily take a vacation until "things settle down" as he phrased it. Lily was furious. She had done nothing wrong, but only Ken knew the truth.

Lily went back downstairs and found a note from Alison that she had gone home. Lily took her backpack and left. She didn't even say good-bye to Tory. Across the street in Carol's office, Lily wrote out a proper retainer. It really cut into her savings. There wasn't much more. She had investments from her royalties and book sales and a retirement account, but a full-out criminal trial would eat that and beyond. She couldn't ask her parents for money. They lived on a retirement pension and social security. Their house was paid off, but it was their home. She would never allow them to mortgage it. Tears welled, but Lily dug her nails into the palms of her hands. *I can't fold up*, she thought. *Whatever happens, I'll find a way.*

Lily said. "I don't understand the sketch and security photo linking me to a bank robbery, and a photo, and Ted's murder."

"You're right," Carol said. "We might be able to attribute the thirteen year-old picture to witness error and the bank camera shot is blurry, but the security camera photo at the victim's apartment is a major problem." Carol stood and held out her hand. "Leave the worrying to me; I'm very good at it."

Lily tried to smile and failed. "Thank you, Carol."

Lily spent the rest of Monday establishing an alibi for March 22, 1995. The most difficult task was explaining it to her parents. They were horrified. "Oh, Lily baby, how could anyone think you would hurt someone? Remember those baby animals you nursed, and the wounded bird?" her mother said, crying.

"It's absolute nonsense," her father said, the anger clear in his voice. "Don't you worry about anything. Whatever you need, just ask."

"Do you want us to come there?" her mother asked.

"There isn't anything you can do right now. Just be ready with that list of names when the police call. They need verification of my whereabouts," Lily said.

"Of course you were there. You helped plan the party. What a ridiculous thought, you robbing a bank and murdering someone. It's horrible," her father said.

"I knew you shouldn't have started writing those gory mysteries. Life mirrors fiction, or something like that." Her mother was close to hysteria.

"Come on Judith, this has nothing to do with her books. Besides, they're more romance than mystery. I'll make some tea. You be careful Lily, and call us every day." Lily heard the extension click.

"I love you, Lily baby," her mother said, sniffing.

"I love you, too, Mom. It's going to be all right, I promise." Lily was very close to tears. They were so precious, and she was very lucky that Bill and Judith Aaron had adopted her. But, they knew nothing about the possibility of a look-a-like relative. The attorney who had arranged the adoption had died five years before, and her parents had received a letter that his family had closed the office. Lily asked her mother if they still had the records.

"Hold on, sweetheart, I'll be right back."

Lily rocked back and forth, gripping the receiver so tightly her hand began to tingle. Morbid, inconceivable thoughts raced through her mind. People were convicted on less, and died after years on death row. How could she prove anything? Just as she was about to scream, her mother returned. The soft, loving voice jerked Lily back from the vortex of a deadly cyclone.

"I have the number, darling."

Lily copied down the information with a shaking hand and, assuring her mother she would be fine, she hung up. Closing her eyes, she breathed deeply, concentrating on the breaths, imagining a sun-drenched meadow of wildflowers and a cool breeze on her face.

Finally, she picked up the phone again and punched in the attorney's number. This was not the time to break down.

"Carol? Lily. My parents are making up a list of people who were at their party. I have a lead to the attorney who orchestrated my adoption. He's dead, but I have a number for the family. Maybe they have records?"

"I should hire you as an investigator when this is over, Lily." Carol took the number and promised that her investigator would check it out immediately.

Lily hated to give up control, but she knew the attorney had more clout than she did. Instead, she checked out the bank robbery on the web. Three men wearing stocking masks had entered the First Regent Bank at 9:05 a.m. and escaped with $450,000 in cash. There was a car waiting for them outside; a woman had been driving, but no one got the license plate. It was in and out...they didn't bother with the safe deposit boxes or the ATM machine, they just took what the tellers had behind the counters. Only three customers were in the store, along with four tellers and a bank manager. No one got hurt.

What had happened to them? Where did they go? How could the woman who drove the car look so much like her that they could match a security camera photo of a woman leaving Ted's home to a photo taken thirteen years ago outside a bank? Lily's head was pounding. There was nothing more she could do, so she changed into her sweat suit and ran four miles to burn off the fear, picking up Chinese take-out on the way home.

CHAPTER 16

Lily's first suspicions surfaced the next day. Ken hadn't called her the previous night, and didn't answer his cell phone. His secretary said he was in court and wouldn't be available until late afternoon. She paced the apartment, worrying her hair. Carol didn't call, and Lily, knowing that it would cost for every minute of every phone call, didn't call her. Finally, the phone rang, but it was Ali wanting to know how she was holding up.

"I'm fine, Ali. Is your asthma under control?" Lily asked.

"Oh yes. Mr. Wilde sent me home yesterday. He said someone would straighten your office and bring in a new computer. It appears the police are hanging on to your old one."

Lily groaned. "I had partly edited story manuscripts on the computer. We'll have to scan them in again, and I'll have to start all over. Then there's all the correspondence and email. I can't replicate that. This is a disaster."

"Mr. Wilde contacted the company's attorneys. They're going to try to get the police to download the files that don't have anything to do with the murder. Oh, this is stupid. You had nothing to do with Ted Warren, so none of your files would be about the murder. This has got me all confused," Ali said, sucking in breath.

"Stop, Ali. This is not something you need to worry about. Play with your grandkids. Go out to dinner with Frank, on me. Have a great evening."

"When are you coming back, Lily?"

"I'm not sure. Right now I'm on mandatory vacation until further notice."

"They have no right to do that."

"Yes, they do, Ali. It's their company, Ted Warren was an employee who died under mysterious circumstances, and I'm an employee who is a suspect. We may not like it or agree with it, but they have the right to do this. I haven't been fired." Lily didn't add "yet."

Ali hung up, still grumbling, and Lily once more dialed Ken's phone. It went to voicemail. Where was he? It was after five o'clock and the court had closed. If she couldn't trust Ken, who could she trust? What was this about trust? They loved each other. They had even talked about a future together, kids, a house in the suburbs. Just because he was tied up at work didn't mean he didn't love her.

"I'm feeling vulnerable for the first time in my life," Lily said aloud. "Well, I'm not a fragile lily, I'm fierce Tiger Lily."

The phone rang. Lily answered quickly, hoping it was Ken.

"Ms. Aaron? This is Detective Dyson."

Lily almost slammed the phone down in frustration. She took a deep breath and said, "Detective?"

"Are you alone?" Dyson asked.

Lily hesitated. "Yes."

"Good! You need to leave the apartment right now. We have some information you should hear. We've already called Ms. Bloom. We're sending someone to get you."

"Wait...why are you telling me to leave my apartment?"

"Just get out of there. A squad car is on the way."

"But—"

The phone clicked, and Lily wondered if the connection was broken.

Lily thought frantically. She was going to be arrested. All her neighbors would see her pushed into the back of a squad car. They would put her in an orange jumpsuit and lock her in a tiny cell. She'd only see her parents through a glass window. The contents of her stomach rose, burning her throat. She dropped the phone and ran for the bathroom. Retching over the toilet, Lily didn't hear the front door open. Only when the shadow loomed behind her did Lily realize that she wasn't alone.

Still crouching, she back peddled across the bathroom floor. She saw brown loafers and jeans, then lifting her head, she saw the shiny black hair. Lily collapsed onto the floor and began to sob.

Ken flushed the toilet and shut the lid, then threw a wet cloth at her. "God, it stinks in here. Wipe yourself off, you're disgusting."

Lily looked up at him in shock. Was this her Ken? He pulled her roughly to her feet and propelled her into the living room. Lily saw the phone still lying on the table where she had dropped it. *What if the connection...? Stall, Lily stall. The cops are coming, just keep him talking.*

Then Lily saw the woman standing by the window, a gun dangling from her hand. It was like looking into a mirror...the same curly blonde hair, the same eyes and features, except for a small scar on her chin. Controlling her shaking voice, Lily mustered all the courage she had left and said loudly, "You're Laurel, aren't you?"

The woman smiled like a Cheshire cat and walked over to Ken. He put his arm around her and smirked. "This has gone very well, Lily. You were so easy to dupe," he said.

Nausea threatened to overtake her again, but Lily fought it back. "Tell me, was Ted Warren one of the bank robbers? And you, Ken, you too?"

Ken shrugged. "Law school is expensive. Then I needed the clothes to go with the fancy law firm, and of course I had to keep Laurel happy."

Lily looked at him in disgust. He laughed. "It was fun, actually...identical twins. How about a threesome for old time's sake? Laurel will be happy to do it, right, darlin'?"

Laurel leaned into him and rubbed his crotch. "Whatever you want, sweetheart. I owe this man big time, dear sister."

"You see, Laurel wasn't as lucky as you, Lily. She got the short end of the stick: a dirt farm on the wrong side of the tracks, an abusive daddy, and then there was Mama and her Jack Daniels. Well, we won't go there, right baby?"

Laurel stretched up to nuzzle his ear.

Bile rose in her throat. Lily hoped the cops were listening on the phone and sending help. All she could do was stall for time and not glance at the table. "I'm sorry, Laurel. I wish I had known about you."

"Yeah, that's sweet. Well, it's too late now, sister dear."

"You killed Ted, didn't you?"

"He was a weak link. You see, the third guy, Phil...well, he got killed in a motorcycle accident years ago. But Ted, he was feeling guilty...wanted to confess his sins, thanks to that religious freak sister of his always dragging him to church. He would have gotten up there and told the world about us."

Ken pulled Laurel closer and squeezed her breast. Lily looked away. "You remember this, don't you, Tiger Lily? You loved it."

Lily swallowed the bile. Her stomach clenched and she wanted to throw up. *Keep them talking.* She forced the words. "How did you find me?"

"Purely by accident," Ken said. "Laurel and I went to a bookstore and there was your picture on a poster for a book signing that Friday night. The rest is history. Get it? The mystery of history, or the history of mystery."

Laurel giggled.

All the book signings were the same. There were so many people, she would never have remembered Ken; she just kept signing books until her hand hurt, smiling by rote, but barely looking up. He must have set up that supposedly chance meeting at Java Cafe, stalking her for weeks; or maybe Laurel set it up, watching her habits and telling Ken. Then there was Ken inviting her to dinner the next day, and eventually telling her he loved her. A few months of ignorant bliss, and now....

"So I was just a convenience," Lily said bitterly.

Ken shrugged. "Laurel and I have been an item for a lot of years. Like I said, it was a trip for me, doing you. You're not exactly a tigress in bed, Tiger Lily, not like Laurel here. You're more a playful pussy cat." He giggled, and it sounded more terrifying than anything Lily had ever heard...the sound of insanity.

Ken went on. "But, hey, I enjoyed every minute. You sure you don't want a threesome...your final farewell, so to speak?"

Lily wanted to pulverize him. He was evil personified. "You're both insane!" she screamed. *Please, someone hear this.*

Laurel stepped forward, waving the gun. "You shut your mouth, sister, or we'll end it now."

Ken reached out and pulled Laurel back. "Easy, easy, sweetheart. She only has a few more minutes of life, let's let her enjoy it."

Lily summoned all her strength to speak. "How are you going to cover up another murder?"

"Oh, this one will be easy." Ken said. "You, as Laurel James, are going to disappear...for a while. Lovely Laurel here will take your place as Lily Aaron. When your alibi holds up, which I will make sure happens, the police will have no choice but to search for Laurel, who, alas, will be found dead in a sleazy motel about five hundred miles from here. And the final clincher, that gun on the bed next to you."

Laurel waved the gun again. "We should let them find her nude. Imagine the cops leering at her body.

Lily shivered and tried to ignore the malice in Laurel's voice. "Is that the murder weapon? So how do I die?"

Ken grinned and pulled a plastic baggie out of his pocket. He waved it at Lily.

She saw a syringe, a spoon, and white powder. Lily swallowed. *Hang on, play for time.* "You'll never pull it off. She won't be able to take my place. I have a job, I have friends, my books."

Laurel smiled. "Simple! You...I...am going to quit my job; too much stress. I'll write to my agent...well, your agent...explaining that this was too, too traumatic, and I am not going to be writing any more murder mysteries."

"Then Laurel...excuse me, Lily...and I will get married and disappear into the sunset," Ken finished.

"What about my parents? They'll never believe I would get married without telling them, or that I would just disappear. They'll file a missing person's report and hound the police."

Ken wrinkled his brow. "Hmm, they might be a problem. Easily resolved...two older people, forgetful; a pilot light not lit, a fire, a road accident...who knows what could happen?"

"You're psychopaths, both of you. You'll never get away with it!" Lily shouted.

"Shut up!" Laurel screamed. "Shut up, shut up, shut up!"

"Easy baby," Ken soothed. "She's just trying to—"

The front door crashed open and cops surged into the room. Lily shrieked as she was thrown to the floor. Deafening gunshots echoed around the room. Ken screamed, "No!"

Lily struggled to look up. A heavy weight lifted from her back and she raised her head. Detective Dyson pulled her onto the sofa. "It's all over, Lily. You're safe."

Lily saw Ken handcuffed, struggling with two burly officers. He was still screaming "No!" as they dragged him out of the apartment. Lily looked down on the floor to see what he was screaming about. She saw herself lying in a pool of blood on her once beautiful Persian carpet. But it wasn't herself she was seeing...it was her identical twin sister, the sister she had never known. Lily pushed off the couch as two EMT's rushed into the room.

"Lily, don't." Dyson tried to stop her.

"Let me go, please. I want to go to her," Lily begged.

Dyson let go of her arm, and Lily crouched beside her sister's head. She was still alive. Their eyes met, and Laurel tried to speak. Lily leaned closer and heard a faint whisper. "I wanted your life, Lily. I wanted...." Her voice trailed off into silence and her eyes clouded over.

Lily looked up. The EMT shook his head and rolled the stethoscope into his pocket. "She's gone. I'm sorry."

Detective Dyson moved Lily over to the sofa, where she sat, sobbing. Detective Dyson and Carol Bloom bracketed her.

"I'm so sorry, Lily," Carol said. She was close to tears. "I never saw it either. Ken was always perfect."

"It was a role," Ann Dyson said.

"Well, he should get an Oscar for it," Lily sobbed, wiping her streaming eyes.

Jamison stood on the other side of the coffee table. "Laurel James was a hard case from childhood. She had a juvenile file and solicitation charges as a teenager."

Lily looked up at him with watery eyes. "She never had a chance. We missed a lifetime together as sisters. My parents would have adopted both of us. This was all because some greedy attorney thought he could make more money selling babies to two families instead of one. It's a damn tragedy, a waste of a life," she raged.

Jamison nodded. "Let's go, Ms. Aaron. The techs have to do their job, and we're in the way."

"I'll stay with you as long as you need me," Carol said. She leaned over and whispered, "As a friend, no billable hours."

Lily turned to the detective. "How did you know?"

"We verified your alibi for thirteen years ago. You couldn't have been robbing a bank in New Mexico when you were in Massachusetts. Besides, the fingerprints the FBI pulled off the car after the bank robbers abandoned it didn't match yours."

"Fingerprints?"

"Well, we've learned that crooks just think they're smart. They make dumb mistakes all the time. There must have been a tear in the glove your sister...uh, I mean Laurel James...was wearing, so they found a usable print on the gear shift."

Lily winced and nodded. "And even identical twins have different fingerprints, so you knew it wasn't me."

"That's right."

"I can't leave my laptop behind; it's my whole life's work."

Jamison nodded and retrieved the computer from the desk, slipping it into the carrying case. Then he shook her hand. "Sorry we had to put you through all this. I'm glad it worked out for you. You're one of the good ones. Besides, my wife is a big fan. She'd have moved me permanently to the guest room if I had arrested you."

Quaking with delayed reaction and nausea, Lily forced a smile, took a copy of her latest book off the shelf, and signed it. "Here, this is for your wife."

Jamison shook his head. "I'm not supposed to do this, but my wife, she'll find out and never forgive me. Thanks, Ms. Aaron, she'll be thrilled."

Dyson rolled her eyes and walked out of the room.

Carol helped her pack some clothes and personal items and whispered, "Don't worry about anything else. Once the apartment is released by the police, we'll get everything packed and you can decide what you want to do with it all."

Lily slung her purse and laptop carrying case over her shoulder. Carol pulled the small suitcase behind her as Lily followed. Lily stopped and turned at the doorway and looked back at the apartment she had called home for five years. It had been her sanctuary, but no longer. She thought of Ken and his betrayal, then Laurel and her wasted life…their lost lives. She never wanted to see it again, especially the bedroom where the sister she had never known had died. Lily would always see the blood on the carpet and hear Laurel's final words, "I wanted your life…."

Gone were the happy memories. These rooms would forever echo with Ken's voice as he told how she would die and disappear. No, Lily would never return.

Her mother's voice whispered in her mind, "Some memories are best forgotten." Lily shuddered and softly closed the door.

***

Lily resigned her job, said good-bye to Alison and Tory, ignoring their tears, and drove to Florida. Her parents met her at the door with open arms and words of comfort, but no questions. The next day Lily and her mother went shopping. Lily replaced all her clothes, because she never again wanted to wear anything Ken had touched or even looked at. For months she reveled in the safety and comfort of her parents' house, sitting on the beach staring at the ocean for days on end. Evenings, she walked the surf, curled up with a book, or watched mindless television sitcoms, for she couldn't handle crime shows anymore.

Lily refused to think further than the next meal; she had no energy left. Completing the book she had started, another mystery was the furthest thing from her mind. The real life experience had tarnished the thrill of creativity in that genre. Her agent told her not to worry, that perhaps she should consider writing something light and funny, or maybe a historical novel. Baking in the sun for days on end, Lily tossed different scenarios around in her mind. No one was pressuring her except herself. It would come, when she, Lily was ready.

True to her word, Carol arranged to have the apartment packed up and the boxes sent to a storage facility. She arranged for books and other items Lily had requested to be sent to Florida, where they languished in the garage.

Lily dutifully went to a therapist every week, where she talked about betrayal and trust. Then one day, she emerged from the cocoon in which she had wrapped herself and spread her wings. She and her father carried the boxes to the Florida room. Together they painted the walls a restful sky blue and installed white book shelves. A blue and green carpet with a swirl design covered part of the tiled floors, and sheer green curtains hung from the bay window. She and her mother went furniture shopping, and within a week, the room morphed into a study. Lily sat on the window seat and looked out at the palms waving in the breeze, framing the lake. The laptop lay unopened on the desk. Lily wasn't ready yet.

A week later, Lily sent her father off to play golf, and took her mother to a spa, treating them to a full day treatment. Afterward, they drove home in silence, Lily deep in her own thoughts.

Judith pulled the car into the garage and got out. "You're glowing, Lily."

Lily stretched. "I feel better, Mom."

Too overcome to speak, Judith put an arm around Lily and pulled her close. "I love you, Lily."

"I know, Mom, I love you, too. And Mom, thanks for adopting me."

Judith Aaron turned away so Lily wouldn't see the tears that welled up, threatening to overflow. Lily knew, though, and pressed her mother's arm.

Inside, Lily went into her study and sat down in front of the laptop. While she waited for it to boot up, she picked up a pen and a legal pad and began to jot down notes. She opened MS Word and a new document. Her fingers moved on the keyboard and words flowed across the screen. Lily had finally accepted what she had to do to expunge the anger and fear that had infiltrated her soul. She read the words on the screen— "Untitled, a novel of love, deceit, murder, and betrayal."

***

A few weeks later Lily and Judith sat outside on the front porch. "So, have you changed your mind about coming up to Cape Cod with Dad and me in July?"

Lily wasn't paying attention...she was looking toward the tennis court where a good-looking, thirty-something guy in whites was practicing serves.

Judith followed Lily's line of vision. "That's the Cooper's son, Mike. You met them; they live down the street. He's visiting from Sarasota for a few weeks. You know he's a—"

"Uh, huh. Mom, I think I'll just wander over to the courts. Is your racket still in the garage?" Without waiting for an answer, Lily went into the garage and glanced around. Two tennis rackets hung on the wall. She took the one with the smaller grip and headed down the driveway.

Judith watched Lily sit down on a bench. After a few minutes Lily said something to Mike Cooper, and as soon as they had retrieved the balls lying around the court, they started volleying back and forth across the net.

"Yes," Judith said, grinning, and pulled out her cell phone. She punched in some numbers and waited. "Ali, I have some good news." Visions of wedding gowns danced in her head.

***

A year later, a new book appeared in bookstores, *Murder in Duplicate* by Lilyann Allon. It received five-star reviews and catapulted onto the bestseller list. According to her agent, the author refused all invitations to do book signings, speaking engagements, or television interviews. However, signed books were available in bookstores across the country, and the author would happily do pre-taped radio interviews.

Lily Aaron Cooper now lived in Sarasota, Florida with her new husband, Michael Cooper, MD., spending her time writing, decorating their home, and traveling. Sometimes unwelcome thoughts sought space in her head, but she forced them away with long walks on the beach at Siesta Key, or a shopping spree on St. Armand's Circle.

Then there was always Michael, the man she trusted and loved. They sat together on the swing in the screened lanai, Michael's hand on her belly. "There they go again." He leaned over and kissed the baby bump. Lily felt the tiny kicks and thought of the twin boys growing in her womb, destined to always be loved and cherished, and never separated.

"I love my boys...my three boys," Lily said.

"Good, because I love my boys and my girl." Michael leaned over and kissed her.

When they came up for air, Lily mused. "I think we'll need a girl or two to make it even."

"I'm all for that, but can we wait a few years, at least until these guys are out of diapers?"

"I guess so, but they had better train early." The setting sun cast a red glow on the water. Lily shifted and settled back against Michael, their hands clasped on the baby bump. She had been given a second chance, and nothing was going to spoil her new life. One of the babies kicked as if reading her mind. She stroked her belly and squeezed Michael's hand. The scarlet sun sank lower, sending orange streaks across the horizon, a pair of tall palms silhouetted against the flaming backdrop. A pair of egrets flew past, heading for a patch of trees to roost for the night. Michael's breath ruffled her hair and she sighed, snuggling closer into his body. He wrapped his arms around her and she felt cocooned and safe, free from the terrifying past.

About the Author

Fran Orenstein, Ed.D., award-winning author and poet, wrote her first poem at age eight and submitted a short story to a magazine at age twelve. Her published credits include: *Gaia's Gift*, a contemporary woman's novel (World Castle Publishing/WCP); three 'tween novels (Sleepytown Press/SP); a young adult fantasy adventure (WCP); a chapter book for younger kids (WCP); and, *Reflections*, a book of poetry for adults (SP).

Her prize-winning short stories and poetry have appeared in various anthologies. She presents writing and publishing workshops at various venues in the Southwest Florida area. Fran's books are available in ebook and paperback format.

Fran has been a teacher, a counselor, written professionally as a magazine editor/writer, and also wrote political speeches, newsletters, legislation, and promotional material while working for NJ State Government for 22 years. She wrote professional papers on gender equity and violence prevention, which she presented at national and international conferences. Fran managed programs for women in gender equity, early education, and disabilities, as well as serving as Special Projects and Disabilities Officer for the AmeriCorps Commission in New Jersey.

She has a BA in Early Childhood Education, a MEd in Counseling Psychology, and an Ed.D. in Child and Youth Studies. Fran is a member of the Florida Writers Association, the Florida State Poets Association, and the National League of American Pen Women.

Visit Fran's World at www.franorenstein.weebly.com for further information on her books, blogs and events.